Mirror Image

Barbra Leslie

Mirror Image

© **Barbra Leslie 2011**

National Library of Australia
Cataloguing-in-Publication entry

Author	Leslie, Barbra, 1940 -
Title:	Mirror image / Barbra Leslie.
Edition:	1st ed.

ISBN: 9780980838510 (pbk.)

Dewey Number: A823.4

Mirror Image is the story of a bizarre relationship between two elderly, neighbouring women.

It is also a statement of the anonymity of many folk living in the suburbs and an observation of the lasting effect of hurtful childhood experiences.

It is a story too of envy and desire that leads one woman to murder, in pursuit of her dream, with a callousness that shocks. The reader follows the gradual growth in some areas of her placid life, none of which is able to change her basic damaged personality.

This story could be happening in the street where you live.

Contents

I

Monica

MONICA carefully adjusted her protective goggles, straightened the plastic apron she used for messy chores (the one with the violets on it), checked that each long sleeve of the jumper was thoroughly tucked into each well-fitting rubber glove, switched on the band saw and slowly but adroitly fed Frank's wrist through the machine.

She was used to the noise. Frank had been using similar saws in the shed ever since they'd moved into the new house, but the pressure that she needed to apply to each side of the limb surprised her a bit. Still, she thought, as she pushed the detached hand aside and slid the forearm along ready for the next cut, she would get used to that in time. Well, butchers do it every day, she reasoned, so why should it prove a problem for her? Even though she was sixty-three years old, she was stocky and strong and even felt a semblance of pride at her ability to use the big machine. Of course she'd watched Frank use it before and was familiar with most of the builder's tools that filled the large shed, but up until now, she'd never actually used much more than an occasional hammer and nail.

Very small sections, she thought. It would take time, but she was a patient woman and methodically continued her task with stoic resignation.

She moved Frank's hand to one side, to be dealt with later, too complicated for now. For a fleeting moment she remembered it holding her own tightly at the funeral but then she thought of the red dress and her jaw clenched tightly as she resolutely continued her grisly task. Half-inch sections, she thought, and as they peeled away she scooped them up and tossed them into the bin she had prepared and placed next to the bench.

Working away, she thought about the red dress. It lay across the back of the lounge sofa. Carefully arranged so as not to crease. One hour's work, she allowed, then she'd shower, do her hair and put it on.

Her mouth filled with saliva at the thought and she swallowed self-consciously. She was a little embarrassed at her own audacity, but excited too. What would happen? What could happen? She was amazed by her own boldness.

Monica had never been known for her boldness. She nearly laughed at the thought, but, aware of the danger of the tool she was using had to smirk wryly instead, keeping her body rigid and her arms and hands firm.

Perhaps leaving home could be called bold, she mused. But no, that was necessity. Getting married so young? No, that was survival. The new house? No, that had been Frank's doing. Frank's doing. Doing Frank. She smiled grimly. No, Doing Frank wasn't bold; she had no choice. But the red dress, she thought proudly, yes, that was bold.

A flush of pleasure crept from her feet throughout her body. She couldn't wait any longer. Flicking the switch that turned off the big saw and throwing the last piece of bone and flesh into the bucket ready for the acid, she realised she was too excited to work safely any more. Then, a cupful at a time, with a steady hand that belied her state of excitement, she added the acid until the contents of the bucket were covered. Placing the lid firmly over the grisly contents she looked at the row of plastic buckets that she'd bought and realised that she would just have to get up early tomorrow and put in a few extra hours.

She carefully wrapped the remains of Frank's arm back

into its green plastic cocoon. Armless. She grinned again. Frank, with his lower-class Yorkshire background used to say "E's 'armless, Bob" or "E's 'armless, old Steve" of his mates at the local. Well, now Frank's armless, she thought, pleased with her own wit and smiled with astonishment as she carefully removed her splattered clothing, gloves last, being careful not to get any yucky stuff on her skin. Astonishment because she was not a witty person; had never been known for her wit.

Or her boldness.

But, witty and bold, after wiping her apron and goggles thoroughly and locking the big shed door, she went inside to prepare for the red dress.

At precisely half past three, resplendent in red, she stepped carefully out through the dinette sliding door on to the back verandah.

II

The estate

THE housing estate that Frank and Monica had chosen for their retirement was unremarkable. The entrance with its name, Sunrise Estate, carved into a high stucco wall settled behind lush lawns and flowering shrubs, did little to indicate that, once inside, there was nothing exceptional, only street after street of similar houses laid out in neat rows. The edge of the estate that ran parallel to the freeway leading to the city, some forty kilometres away, had a fine buffer of native vegetation to cut down the noise and it was the higher side of the group of two hundred or so medium-priced houses. It was along this edge that Frank and Monica chose their block, the frontage of which looked out over the entire estate.

On one side of their home, to their right, was a two-storey cream brick house built a couple of years before they arrived. Perhaps a display home, finished so early and sporting well-established shrubs in the front yard. On the other side, which was still an empty block when they chose their own, some four years ago, had been built a red brick single-storey family home.

Their own house was also single-storeyed and with a back verandah running right along the full length of the home to shield late afternoon sunshine.

All the blocks had low brick front fences, with tiny built-in letter boxes, and similar low brick walls separating the houses. These small walls only went as far as the front of the houses then changed to higher colourbond fences which gave each backyard a modicum of privacy.

According to the agent, the two-storey house had been occupied by a retired school principal, who kept to herself and should cause no trouble

The red-brick house to their left, finished not long after their own, belonged to a young couple with two children; a boy, seven, and a girl of two.

Monica and Frank in their retirement didn't want noisy neighbours but the planning of the houses worked to their advantage with their own garage side butting against the double garage of the young couple, leaving quite a distance between the two homes.

Most of the houses in the estate were in fact owned by younger couples, nearly all with children. There were only a dozen or so different designs available, two being double-storeyed. The interiors were practically identical, but with some designs built in reverse, a front porch added here and there. From the road the new suburb simply seemed tidy and pleasant.

From the air though, should one ever see it from that perspective, the parallel lines of streets were lined with box after box of repetitive shapes, a small suburb within the larger suburb that surrounded it.

Frank and Monica had never owned a house before. They had lived their entire married life of forty-five years in the one rented house, across the other side of the city from the new estate.

Monica and Frank were not a happy couple. They were not unhappy either, simply complacent. But there was no laughter in their house. During their years of marriage they had grown slowly, miserably together into the ageing unit of acceptance they now occupied.

Things had not always been that way. Once, long, long ago, they had believed they were in love and both carried expectations of a long and fruitful life. Frank, a builder, seemed guaranteed of employment and a reasonable income. He had a vague grand plan of owning his own building empire, but the plan was doomed by his own lethargy and pigheadedness, before fate stepped in and destroyed any remnants of success when his only son, Peter, was killed in a tragic accident in his late teens.

Frank, anyway, was not a very likeable character. He was moody, sullen and introverted; had been ever since a child and the loss of his only son had not improved his attitude towards life, his peers and his wife.

Monica, withdrawn and dowdy, had in reality only married Frank because she thought nobody else would ever ask her. She'd been a plain child who had grown into a plain young woman and not only was she without the beauty to attract young men of merit and desire, she also lacked the personality which draws people together.

Her childhood, spent in a lower-class working environment, with one brother and one sister, had been devoid of inspiration and encouragement. Her mother was a self-absorbed drinker and her father, driven to distraction by his selfish wife and the financial drain of alcohol and three children, worked two jobs to meet the bills and was seldom home, until he died of a heart attack when Monica was only fourteen. The siblings had little concern with each other, each having withdrawn into themselves behind a myriad of barriers in order to survive the screaming brutality of their drunken mother.

At fifteen, when allowed to leave school, Monica left home. Before her birthday even came around she had organised a job for herself in a small nursery in the adjoining district helping to pot the herbs and flowers that brought in the customers.

In the city, a half-hour bus trip from the nursery, she had come across a boarding house where she could rent a quiet, simple room for a pittance and there, alone and away from the explosive temper of her mother, she found a great sense of peace and control. As the eldest child it had always fallen to her to do the shopping for the family and it was on one of her bi-weekly trips to the city that by chance she had found this haven, a two-storey building with rented rooms, a shared kitchen and three shared bathrooms. After a few attempts at using the kitchen, however, she found it difficult to have to talk to whoever else was there at the time, and as soon as her small wage could afford, she bought a gas-burner and later, a small fridge, and cooked and ate by herself in her tiny room.

So much was her need to leave home after her father's death that she cared little for her brother and sister's position. Three and six years younger than herself respectively, and left in the dubious care of the unreliable mother, they needed her alliance, but to her somewhat surprised relief she felt nothing for them and only saw them occasionally if they came to the nursery to say hello. She never went back to her home again, so afraid of her mother's wrath at losing her main care-giver and worker, but settled, happy and alone, into her drab little room.

She treasured the tranquillity of her new home. Nobody called her a stupid cow, which had been her mother's name for her for as long as she could remember. "Get those dishes done, you stupid cow", or "Isn't tea ready yet, you stupid cow". Even when on occasion she brought a good report card home from school (never brilliant, but sometimes good) her mother's response was "And where's that going to get you, you stupid cow, just look at you". So she had withdrawn behind a wall in her mind where she was safe from names and taunts and there she happily stayed, flat, dull and lifeless, but safe.

Two years after beginning work at the nursery where she was a quiet and reliable little worker, she met Frank who had recently finished his apprenticeship and had been sent to collect some plants for his boss.

"G'day woman", he smiled at her. "I'm looking for half a dozen flowering shrubs. What can you show me?"

Thrilled at being called a woman, Monica, at seventeen, blushed as she took him through the nursery, pointing out specific plants. She felt very small, and feminine even, to

14

her surprise, walking beside this big, strong young man and was pleased when he told her he'd be around the following week for more.

He was much older than her, she guessed, and not what you'd call good-looking really, but nice-looking, she decided, with his big nose and square jaw. He reminded her of her dad. But he would never be interested in her, she thought. Too young and too plain.

At seventeen Monica was actually quite attractive. Although her fair hair which she wore to the shoulder was straight, it was always immaculately clean and shone in the sun. She had a roundish face which was mostly devoid of expression, but when she did smile her green eyes became beautiful and her soft, young mouth would be inviting and tempting to any young man. She was shortish and plump. Not fat, just nicely plump and her flawless young skin tended to make one think of ripe fruit.

Frank was certainly taken with her. Immediately. He loved her deference to him which made him feel manly and strong. Certainly he thought she was older than she was, but her reaction to him had not been lost on his ego.

Women generally didn't blush and fumble in his presence. Most of the beautiful young women he met tended to ignore him somewhat or treat him like a brother.

He had slept with a few women, the desperate ones, but no-one so far that he genuinely liked.

The following week he returned, determined to ask her to the movies if he felt the same way on a second look. And he did and she went.

Within weeks they were going steady, both comfortable in each other's company. No demands, no expectations, no jealously, no fights. Nothing to fight about really, both of them being pliable and undemanding.

On Monica's eighteenth birthday, at his suggestion, they went back to her tiny room and made love for the first time.

Monica knew absolutely nothing about sex and was

surprised at his passion, his pleasure and his gratefulness. For herself, she found it slightly painful, awkward and basically pretty boring. She liked afterwards best, when Frank held her in his big arms and stroked her hair and told her he loved her.

And so it went until Monica became pregnant at nineteen. After two years of easy company together they had no problem deciding to get married. They were a pretty solid unit by then, Frank getting his sex whenever he wanted, Monica getting companionship and love, both of them placidly accepting the needs of the other. Neither thought that there would be or could be anything more in a relationship and when they married in the Registry Office the pair of them blindly accepted that they would be together until death.

Mr Jason, who owned the nursery and had become fond of his quiet, hard-working employee, gave Monica away. One of Frank's building mates stood up for him. Monica didn't even tell her mother, not wanting a maudlin, drunken scene, but secretly managed to bring her brother and sister to the ceremony where they sat quietly fiddling until they could leave, neither of them caring much whether their sister, whom they hardly knew, got married or not.

Monica and Frank were good enough parents to their son when he was born, providing a solid stable home for him to grow in. Peter, though, was a bright likeable lad with many friends and good grades at school. He didn't want to be a carpenter and had many good job options available to him. Although he loved his parents and was grateful for his solid, quiet upbringing, he was secretly ashamed of his mother and father and their lack of passion for life. At eighteen, half-way through a new computer course for bright, gifted youngsters, he was out with the fast set of students that he spent his time with when the car in which he was passenger left the road and hit a tree at high speed. He died on impact.

Monica and Frank both dealt with the accident in their own quiet way. Frank drank more than usual for a couple of years and Monica turned to television where she could lose herself in the undemanding storylines on the screen.

Their life had since plodded along quietly and without incident as they both grew slowly older.

Although Frank took an extra job here and there to supplement his gambling money (his one pleasure)he had stayed with the one company his whole working life, managing to keep his employment when the company changed hands several times and eventually grew into a big corporation that built entire housing estates. They owned, in fact, the estate where the new house sat and Frank got a good deal on the place with his super when he turned sixty-five.

With the house paid for outright the couple could manage well enough on the pension. Frank's love of the racetrack was limited now, except when he took an occasional small subbing job, but generally speaking, not much had changed financially for the couple.

Monica had stopped working at the nursery when she married Frank at nineteen. Although she had been pregnant with Peter at the time, the marriage was in the offing anyway as the young couple were comfortable enough together to realise that not much better would probably come the way of either of them.

Retirement, per se, meant little to Monica as she had always stayed at home since the marriage, first of all to care for Peter then, after his death, to cook, clean and sit in front of the tele for hours on end, placid, sad and withdrawn.

Frank, on the other hand, was pleased with retirement, not having to rise at 6.30am each day to face repetitive work and boredom.

He'd accrued a good set of tools over the years and a large collection of wood scraps from jobs. He fancied himself spending his retirement making wooden toys in the large shed he'd put at the back of the block. Rocking horses he dreamed of, all colours, shapes and sizes. Perhaps even, should he get good enough, horses for a carousel, intricate and beautiful.

His first two rocking horses stood unpainted in the shed, waiting for their undercoat. Not bad pieces either, for a beginner.

At first, after the move, Frank would sometimes amble around the new estate and catch up for a chat with some of his old workmates who were still finishing off some of the houses. But as the estate filled and the houses were completed there was less and less chance of finding a workman whom he knew. His old drinking spot, a three-hour drive away now, had to be replaced with a new hotel about fifteen minutes drive from the house. Here he'd sometimes have a few beers and a bet on the TAB, but the unknown patrons seemed less friendly than those at his old pub and he was less inclined to stay for long periods of time.

Monica was no help. No company at all, really. Okay for tea time and a bit of telly at night, like in his working days, but a dead loss during the afternoons when she would want to watch her beloved soap operas. So this was the time, the empty hours on most days, that he spent in his shed, gradually building the two horses. Soon he would paint them. The thought excited him. Building he knew, but decorating was a whole new thing and he kept putting it off, savouring the anticipation and unsure quite how he was going to go about it.

Frank didn't have any close mates. Some of the guys at work always seemed to hang out together and sometimes he'd heard them planning fishing trips or footy outings. He was never included and he never approached them for an invitation. He wasn't a shy man, but nor was he really approachable. Since his son's death he had become more and more insular; fine for an occasional beer at the pub, but not the sort of bloke you'd want to spend your Saturdays with. Frank never felt he was missing out on

18

anything. He had his home and his wife and his job and he figured that was his lot. Even when the job ended he was still sort-of satisfied with his life.

And so, basically, was Monica. Sometimes, at the shops, she would look at the other women, the smartly dressed, competent, beautiful women with style, and wonder what their life was like. Not with envy or bitterness or even real curiosity, simply with an acknowledgment that they were different. There were also many women at the shops like herself; plain, dumpy women, dressed in trackies or an old skirt and a cardie, trudging their way through the mall as they did through life. Wearing their acceptance of their lot on their bland faces.

The whole world, it seemed to Monica, consisted of Them and Us. And accepted this as so.

Shopping centres were as familiar to her as her own home. She had always shopped. First for mother and the family, trying to get the most value out of the meagre money left after the alcohol was bought. Then for herself when she left home, still always limited by shortage of cash after paying rent out of her small salary. Then for herself and Frank, money a little freer, but still a worry with Frank's gambling eating into the pay packet every week.

She knew where to get the best bargains, the cheaper brands. Where food was concerned she had learned over the years how to make a reasonable meal from the cheaper cuts, bake her own biscuits, cakes and pudding and even preserve the fruits of the season while they were cheap and plentiful.

As far as personal items went, clothes and toiletries, she had long ago given up ever going for a look inside the smart shops. "Those shops", she called them in her mind. Those shops, with smart salesgirls who, after one dismissive glance, turned their attention elsewhere.

Once, many years ago, not long after she and Frank were married, she'd gone into one of those shops to look for a dress for the occasional dinner or party to which they were sometimes invited.

With the courage of youth and looking forward to a wedding they'd been asked to attend, she thought she'd try something different and actually went into one of the little boutiques. There were only two outfits in the front window and a few glamorous accessories draped over driftwood (most unusual) and once inside she was surprised to find the interior stocked as sparsely as the window. The dress shops she usually frequented were jam-packed with rows and rows of hangers and circular racks with ten or so pieces of the one design, catering for any size you could want. This fancy shop, however, only had one example of each piece, some displayed on mannequins and the rest carefully spaced out along racks running down each side of the shop.

The smart navy blue and white trimmed shirt-dress in the window was what had drawn her inside the place, but there were no others to be seen once there and she had to approach the small counter at the back of the shop and ask the stony-faced woman who lifted her head with disdain just how much was the dress in the window.

"Quite a good purchase, that one," she said. "This year's newest label and with red accessories available." She glanced at Monica's plain skirt and jumper, knowing instantly their value and named a price so far out of Monica's reach that the poor girl actually gasped: "What?" And, flushed and embarrassed, found herself unable to move.

"Woollies has a similar range," the salesgirl offered with a certain amount of pity. "The cut's not as good and of course the fabric is synthetic, but they're sure to have something in your size."

Monica, a little overweight for her height at 21, turned and left the shop. She had been told. In just a few words she had been told exactly where she stood in life. Inside herself, she'd always known really. "Stupid cow", her mother used to call her, and even though the smart shop assistant hadn't said it, Monica could feel the thought aimed at her back like a placard as she quickly left the dreaded shop to walk back into her own world of the mall, where she melted into the crowd of shoppers and could breathe again.

She never entered, or even contemplated entering, one of those shops again.

Them and Us.

The housing estate seemed to be somewhere in the middle of Them and Us. However Monica felt quite at ease with their inclusion in the new estate. From the front, at least, their house looked every bit as good as all the others and their car, a late model Commodore, was not out of place in the plethora of vehicles that cruised the streets.

Very few people strolled the footpaths of the estate. Dozens of children of various ages roared around the district on bikes, roller blades and skateboards, but there was only an occasional mother pushing a stroller as far as adult participation was concerned. The younger majority of home-owners whipped in and out of their roll-a-door garages several times a day, but other than that were seldom to be seen. Monica herself, in fact, had never walked the streets, always leaving to shop in the car and returning the same way.

The Nelsons, their neighbours on the left, had once invited them in for a barbecue just before Christmas. Several of the other neighbouring families were there, all younger couples with children. They were a pleasant enough bunch but Monica, in particular, had nothing in common with the other women and spent the evening sitting quietly on the edge of the group who chattered away happily about schools and children and local gossip. She wished fervently that they hadn't come and slipped away as soon as the meal was finished and she could take her empty salad bowl from the laden table, with the excuse of a bad back. The fact that Monica didn't drink made matters worse. The other women were all drinking champagne and wine and as the afternoon turned to evening she was ignored more and more as they became louder and laughed uproariously at this or that comment.

Their neglect of her was not malicious or obvious, in fact each one of them had made some effort to speak to her and include her in the conservation. It was difficult for everyone and when Monica went home her hosts were as happy about it as she was. Frank fared a little better and stayed on a bit longer, drinking beer with the boys and sharing in topics such as sport or politics. He was by far the oldest one there and felt out of his depth with the vehemence and passion of his fellow drinkers.

"Not a bad old chap" was the joint opinion when he left, but the group all knew that the pair would not be invited again and the Nelsons felt as if they'd done their bit as neighbours and could happily forget the old couple in the future.

Monica's reluctance, in fact refusal, to drink had curtailed quite a bit of social life during Frank's working days when there was a company picnic or dinner. She had decided when she left home that she would never touch the stuff after seeing what it had done to her mother and the rest of the family, and understandably so. Frank understood that but she didn't have the type of personality that saves non-drinkers in social situations that seemed to revolve around alcohol. Some people could chatter and laugh and keep their listeners amused without the help of a drink but Monica wasn't one of them, shy to the extreme and lacking in both personality and will. She was in fact only comfortable with Frank. Comfortable and safe.

Even when Peter had been at junior school and, out of duty, she'd attended parents' meetings, she never held office, volunteered for a committee or really made any input into the group. She could always be counted on for scones, cake, jam and preserves for fund raisers but other than that she gave nothing to the group. Needless to say, she had no close women friends. Ever. She had been alone since her father had died and alone she stayed, other than

Frank. She was not unhappy that way; she never missed the pleasures that are found in friendship and never looked for any companionship outside her marriage.

So the estate suited Monica very well. There was an anonymity about it that made her feel comfortable. Sure, every now and then there would be a party somewhere, with blinking lights and loud music, or the more common barbecue, laughter and noise and smoke drifting up and down the roads, but inside her own small boundaries, either with Frank or without, Monica was content.

During their years at the estate Monica had seen very few elderly people about the place. Her neighbour on the other side, whose name she didn't know, was old. Older than herself anyway. The agent had told them that she was retired and sometimes Monica might see her leaving her house in her car, grey-headed and insular. Both Monica and Frank had no desire to meet the woman and had made no moves in that direction, even though she was more their own age and approachable one would think. She had similarly never called upon them, not even when they'd first moved in. It seemed a given that both owners of the neighbouring houses keep to themselves, unknown and uncared for in their own little boxes.

III

The verandah wall

One hot summer washing morning, probably about four years after Frank and Monica moved into the new house, annoyed with the same old make-shift line and the dust beneath her slippers, Monica suddenly decided to look into the neighbouring back yard. Small but well-established trees were visible over the high fence, but other than that Monica had no idea what the yard contained. It couldn't possibly be as bad as theirs, she thought.

This was a daring move. What if she were caught peering over the fence? What would she say? She hesitated a moment, glancing around the shambles of their own yard, still bare but for Frank's big shed, his piles of untidy timber stacked along the verandah and a pile of wooden boxes left over from the move. The washing hung sadly from a nylon line attached to a post by the shed and another about a metre from the neighbour's fence.

Quickly, before she changed her mind, she took one of the wooden crates, checked it for spiders and placed it against the fence.

Hesitantly now, but having made her mind up, she stood on the box, grasping the sharp top of the fence with both hands, and peered over.

From where she stood about half-way along the fence she could see a tidy well-managed garden full of shrubs and small trees, some of which hid the back of the house altogether from her vantage point. Two small vegetable plots, unused for a year or two she would think, abutted the fence and a small compost heap, sprouting a stalk or two, sat in the back corner. She was unable to see the verandah, the roof of which was visible from her own, and after a little hesitation she moved the box along the fence, virtually between the two verandahs and stepped up for a quick look.

What she saw took her breath away.

The L-shaped two-storey house was cream brick, like their own, with the hollow of the "L" facing their fence. The house came within about a metre of the fence so that when Monica lifted her eyes over the top of the iron she felt that she was virtually within that verandah.

And what a verandah it was.

Oh, it was beautiful!

She swallowed lustfully.

It was like a fairy tale.

The verandah was immaculate. The floor had been laid with blue-and-white patterned tiles and at the nearest end stood two beautiful palms in large blue ceramic pots which matched the blue of the tiles. The entrance to the house, a sliding glass door exactly like her own, was clean and shiny, reflecting the shrubs that had blocked Monica's earlier view. These shrubs, some in flower – yellow and red – had been planted in a curve from the fence, leading gently back to the other side of the block where the garage abutted the farthest side of the house. The small area between shrubs and verandah was soft green lawn and the well placed plants and trees seemed to extend the verandah into a soft pleasant landscape that hid much of the iron fence from the house.

Carefully placed between the glass doors and the side of the house was a small, round glass table on black wrought-iron legs, with a black wrought-iron chair tucked neatly beneath it. The chair had a small velvet cushion on it in blue, to match the pots and the tiles. On the table sat a beautiful china pot, the like of which Monica had never seen. "Grecian" popped immediately into her head, but she really had no idea what a Grecian pot would actually look like.

But the most amazing thing, the most beautiful thing of all was the white couch, a two-seater leather. Soft and comfortable, it sat along the return wall of the verandah, set in a bit from the edge to obviously protect it from the weather. Another, smaller, round glass table with wrought-iron supports sat between the lounge and the edge of the verandah.

Monica had never seen a real-life glass table before. Sometimes, in magazines, but not REAL. Not next door, over the fence.

There were two cushions on the couch. Velvet. One the same blue as the tiles. One bright red. The same red, in fact, as the geranium in full bloom that was planted in the lawn at the end of the tiled floor where the table sat.

A secret and solitary place.

A vision.

Monica held her breath for a second before slowly stepping down from her box. She stood facing the fence for some time, unmoving, then slowly turned to face her own verandah and backyard.

What a dismal mess. Her own long verandah, running in line with the one next door, was a shambles. Frank's wood, the old boxes and a couple of broken plastic chairs cluttered the length of it, with dust and dry leaves piled high against every surface.

She stood there for some time, her face blank, then slowly went inside her own sliding door to the dinette and kitchen.

To be fair, she thought, she and Frank had spent a lot of time and effort getting the front garden up to scratch. With both of them withdrawn and lost in their own lethargy it had taken practically a year to topsoil and level the front for a small stretch of lawn with a few native ground covers for a border. All of the front yards in the estate were very small, but very tidy, and it was important to both Frank and herself that their garden "belonged" with the rest.

Still, she thought, methodically cutting and chopping for a casserole for tea, it would be nice… Grimly she smiled. As if.

Next morning, though, seemingly drawn by a magnet, Monica had to climb on to the wooden box for another peek. Oh, she thought, if I could just sit on that couch in the afternoon sun. No television, no anything, just sit and look and be. How she loved those tiles; so clean, so fresh, so beautiful. She found that her hands were hurting, so tightly was she gripping the top of the iron fence, and, coming back to reality she hopped down, went inside and turned on the tele. She slumped into her vinyl lounge chair and stared at the screen, but the vision of that verandah filled her head and she saw nothing of the morning programs but was lost in a dream, a wish, a deep longing.

The next day, going down to Frank's shed to collect his dirty overalls for the wash, she noticed, for the first time, a pile of cream bricks stacked along one wall. She never really took much notice of the shed's interior, Frank's territory, but remembered seeing the bricks left over from the house and some talk of a barbecue being built out the back.

When next she hung the washing out to dry, hating the back yard with a vengeance that surprised her, she suddenly had a flash of genius. A thought so bold that she bit her lip and made it bleed. Sucking on the blood she went inside and made a cup of coffee, which stung her lip and somehow, cemented by the pain, a resolve to have her way and change her life took hold.

Over tea that night, when Frank was feeling contentedly full and mellow after his pre-dinner beer, Monica said, more firmly than she would ever have imagined, "Frank I was looking at those cream bricks today and thinking."

"Yeah, well," said Frank, "I don't know about a bloody barbecue. When would we ever use it?"

"Yes, yes you're right," she grabbed at his answer. "I was actually thinking of something else."

"What on earth else?" said Frank, peering over his glasses at her, astonished, in a way, that his wife could even have an idea.

"I'd like to brick off one end of our back verandah," she said, strongly, "for a place to sit out of the wind."

Astounded, Frank laughed.

"A place to sit out of the wind! When do you ever sit outside I'd like to know. There's no wind in the lounge by the tele."

"I've been thinking about it a lot," she retorted, sure of herself now. "I'd like to start planting out the backyard and I'd like a place to sit in the afternoons. You can have the rest of the verandah for your stuff."

Frank buttered a piece of bread, thought for a while and waggling the knife at her, said slowly "Now let me get this clear. You want a wall halfway along the verandah."

"Not halfway," she interrupted, "only to the end of the dinette door. Here." She turned to indicate. "It would stop the draught coming in and I could decorate it a bit."

Decorate, thought Frank, whenever had his wife ever, ever thought about decorating. Their two homes only ever had the necessary furniture. This woman with whom he had lived for forty-odd years didn't even decorate herself. Decorate? Perhaps she was still going through the menopause – he'd heard that sometimes made them funny. Or was it old age? Was she going loony or summat?

"Yes," she continued, more sure of herself now. Determined. "Yes, decorate it. And plant a garden."

Frank was out of his depth. He had no idea what to do. Never had he seen his wife quite like this. Even her mouth looked different. Firm even. He became a little apprehensive.

"I'm not sure if there's enough bricks. I'll have to check."

"Have a look tomorrow," she said as if the whole matter had been agreed to, and began clearing the table. "Perhaps you would like a piece of lemon-meringue pie while you watch a movie?"

Frank nodded, pleased the odd conversation was over. She'd probably forget all about it. He looked for a minute at her back as she scraped the dishes at the sink, but there was nothing there to explain what had just happened. He took the plate of pie that she had put in front of him and went into the lounge to watch the football show. She joined him after she'd finished the dishes and sat quietly in her chair staring blankly at the television. Frank glanced at her again, but there was nothing unusual about her behaviour and by the time the show was over he'd forgotten the entire conversation.

The following evening as he tucked into an exceptionally nice beef roast Monica leaned across the table towards him and asked: "Are there enough?"

Enough what, thought Frank, Enough potatoes? Enough carrots? What is she on about? Then lifting his eyes and seeing her face before him, lips tight, he suddenly remembered the bricks.

Oh God, he realised, she really means it. Stupid cow. What a ridiculous idea. But she meant to be answered, that was plain by the look on her face.

"Enough I reckon, but are you sure about this. Seems odd to me to split the verandah into two."'

"It'll be nice," she said, settling back into her chair smiling. "And I'll start the garden. The shrubs should be in by autumn. It's the best time to plant."

Ah, what harm can it do, thought Frank. He'd never seen her quite so set on an idea, and the backyard certainly needed some work, which he didn't intend putting much time into. She was the one who'd worked in a nursery and it was only fitting that she do the yard.

Money had been set aside for the plants but after the front yard was finished they'd both sort-of let it go. It certainly was an eye-sore. Besides he felt a little guilty about his stack of untidy timber. He wanted to keep it dry but didn't want to clutter the shed. He reckoned he could whip a wall up in a couple of days if he set his mind to it and if it kept the old girl happy what did it matter.

"I'll start it Tuesday."

"That'll be nice," she said, and with a knowing smile offered "perhaps we could have an early night tonight, there's not much on."

Aha, thought Frank, pleased. Nooky. It'd been a while. His groin twitched in anticipation. Sex did not play a big part in their lives anymore. Going on seventy, Frank wasn't as needy as he used to be. Monica just plain wasn't interested. Never had been. Had to do it because Frank wanted her to, but never really liked it. Didn't dislike it either. Didn't care.

When they first met and Frank was a virile twenty-three-year-old he'd been at her all the time. She'd been a virgin still and he was really the first proper boyfriend she'd ever had. Twice, since she'd been working at the nursery, she'd accepted an invitation to the movies, 'dates' I suppose you'd call them, with younger boys, but didn't like the fumbling and kissing that went along with them. Frank had been different. He was already sexually experienced at twenty-three and was in no hurry to push her too far too quickly. He had liked her placid acceptance of himself. In fact he valued it highly. He was not a bright fellow and his needs were small. Although he was a big man and somewhat attractive in a country-sort-of-way, he'd found difficulty with conversations with previous girlfriends and was uneasy eating at the restaurants they frequented and the parties that they invariably wanted to go to. This little piece, he had realised, although not a beauty, was quite a find. Independent already at eighteen, a good little worker by the looks of it and as unsophisticated as he was. Good tits, too.

Since the very first time when he took her, more gently than even he thought he was capable of, on the single bed in her little room, she had never ever said "no" to his advances. Not even when she was pregnant with Peter. She was a placid lover but satisfied his needs and he'd been content enough throughout their life together.

After Peter's tragic death, however, the broken-hearted couple grew apart into their own unbearable pain. Instead of it bringing them closer, both physically and emotionally they became two human units functioning side by side instead of the comfortably bonded beings they had been before, and sex became less important to Frank. Sometimes he would meet his body's needs under the shower in preference to facing the sadness and pain of his wife's face.

Never had Mon initiated sex before. Never. Not once. It had always been Frank's responsibility and domain. So the suggestion of an 'early night' was not only a surprise but a titillation in itself. Frank moved on his chair and lifted his weight from one cheek to the other. He slipped his left hand under the table and adjusted his balls. Christ, he thought, what a turn-on. He looked across at his wife who was carefully and deliberately slicing through a freshly baked chocolate cake.

She hadn't really changed much over the years, he noted. The light brown hair had kept its colour really well. A bit of grey, here and there, but not like his own, silver and sparse. She was a little overweight, always had been, but had kept her shape pretty well for an old girl. Her waist was still pretty trim, considering, and the ample breasts above it only served to enhance its shape. Frank swallowed lustfully. He felt his penis move within the confines of his trousers. You little beauty, he thought, I'll build 'er half a dozen brick walls at this rate!

"Cream?" she asked.

Cream, he thought, I'll pour it all over 'er and lick it off. Mon suggesting a fuck, he couldn't believe his ears. There was a glint in her eye that he didn't remember ever seeing before. Not even when they were young. Young. That was a while ago, but hell, he felt pretty young at the moment.

"Later," he said grabbing the moment. "Come now, Mon. Come to bed now." And getting up and taking her hand, he led her to the bedroom, leaving plates and food on the table, uncovered and unheard of.

Monica followed like a child, his big hand firm and strong about her own. She felt quite a sense of power; a new experience for her – an aging woman of sixty-four, beginning to wrinkle despite her roundness. Somewhere, sometime along the flatness of her life she'd neglected this gift that suddenly became an obvious bargaining weapon. Power. She felt a strange compassion for her husband. A kind of pity. And before he entered her she took his penis in her hand and gently helped him to a full erection.

Well, what a business! Frank was so overcome he couldn't last the distance. But what an event. He lay next to the wife he didn't know anymore. He reached out tenderly and stroked her hair. She turned to smile at him, a smile he'd never seen before. Seductress and child combined. Hesitantly he ran his rough hand down and across her body, soft and warm. He felt another stirring between his legs. Never, never had he been able to do it twice. He was a oncer. Before the magic was lost he lifted his weight on top of her and thrust more vigorously than he thought he was capable of.

What a night.

Life changed for them both. Monica secretly acknowledged her newly discovered power and Frank quite obviously, laid himself open to her wishes and desires.

Next day, whistling, Frank began the wall.

It took some time. He was getting older and slower. With the shopping for cement and sand and cutting bricks in half, he only had a few layers finished by nightfall.

Monica watched him toil through the kitchen window as she cleared away last night's dishes and prepared his lunch and his dinner. She felt good. She felt happy. She felt excited. She would have her wall and even, dare she speed ahead of herself, she would have a blue-and-white tiled

33

floor. She knew what to do. She knew how to get it. She hummed happily to herself as she prepared the tuna mornay for tea and thought she would go shopping tomorrow and perhaps take a quick look in the tile shop by the mall. Just in case. Just in case she might see something similar.

Or the same!

She held her breath for a moment, stunned at the thought. The same. Well, why not? Tiles are tiles. Anybody can buy them. The concept frightened her a little. Slow down. She would just have a look around and see what was available.

"Frank," she called through the screen door, "would you fancy a cup of coffee?" For the cost of the tiles.

"Thanks, Mon."

"No trouble," she said, bringing two cups out to the verandah. They squatted on the cement leaning against the wall of the house. "Could do with a couple of comfy chairs out here," said Monica, "or a couch." Breathless at her own daring.

"Um" said Frank, occupied with the laying of bricks.

Still, it had been said.

IV

The red dress

It seemed to have taken Monica forever to find that red dress. Only three days, really. She'd trudged from store to store, looking always for reds and rifling through them impatiently, hoping the right one would be there. But there was nothing even similar. No swirled bottom, no graceful neckline, no sleeve with a draped cuff.

Frustrated and annoyed, Monica even tried the smaller shops along the main road. Nothing there either.

One day, the fourth, trudging past one of "those shops", a flash of red caught her eye, and turning, she saw a shop assistant through the doorway, carrying a hanger above the splash of red.

Much stronger now in herself since the beef roast, but still a bit hesitant, Monica stepped into the shop.

"Can I help you, Madam?"

"That dress, that red dress," said Monica, "may I see it please. I'm looking for a particular shape."

The assistant held the dress up, displaying the flared hem and the draped cuff.

"Oh, yes," breathed Monica, "that's the one."

She clenched her lips tightly and held her knees firm to stop them shaking.

"I'd like to try it on," she breathed. Putting her handbag firmly on the counter. A statement. I will not leave.

"This particular one, Madam," said the saleswoman,

"may be a bit small." Eyeing her weight against the soft fabric of the dress.

"I'll try it on," said Monica, already committed to bravery beyond anything she had ever known. And she did, struggling to wiggle it down over her large bosom and heavy thighs.

"How are we, in there?" Called the girl.

We are all right, thought Monica in the dressing room, but the bloody dress is too small. Reluctantly and with some difficulty she manoeuvred it back over her head and put it back on the hanger.

"Do you have this in the next size," she called, flustered and ashamed.

"No, Madam, but we can get one in for you if you wish."

"Yes, please," said Monica "and what is the price?"

"Four hundred and seventy."

Still in the change room Monica turned red. Four hundred and seventy dollars! On the pension! Frank would have a fit, despite being so pliable over the last few weeks. What could she do? She couldn't stay in the change room forever.

Resolutely she stepped out from the booth and faced the salesgirl. "Yes, order one for me, please."

"May I take Madam's measurements," the girl asked politely, "it will help with the order."

"Of course," answered Monica, standing as tall and as straight as possible, embarrassed beyond bearing. "And how long will it take?"

"Three days, Madam."

"Fine," said Monica, collecting her bag from the counter and starting towards the door..

"Madam," said the shop assistant rather sharply, "we'll need a deposit and an address and phone number."

"Well, of course." Monica pulled out her purse and looked inside. All she had was sixty-three dollars for housekeeping for the rest of the week.

"Fifty dollars?" asked Monica, dreading that it would not be enough, falling back into her old, old fear.

"Yes, Madam," was her answer, and with her receipt and address given, Monica took leave of the shop feeling extremely pleased with herself, and proud. Yet another new feeling emerging.

Directly across the mall from the boutique was a classy little coffee house. Monica headed straight for it, desperately in need of a sit-down and a nice coffee. She sat in the first empty booth. A waitress came and she ordered a white coffee.

What sort of white coffee?

"Cafe latte, flat white, cappuccino?" Monica guessed at a flat white and slowly sipped it while she pondered on what she had just done. Slowly she calmed. He would just have to lump it. She'd never asked for much, all these years. And him with his gambling and his beer.

Feeling better, she went to the counter to pay the bill. Four dollars fifty! For a coffee! She paid quickly from the remaining ten-dollar note and left.

She sat in the car in the car park for nearly an hour before driving home. She would have to tell Frank. There was not enough money left for food.

Over dinner, quiche and salad with a steamed golden syrup pudding she quietly said "I bought a new dress today."

"Um," said Frank, busy with his pudding.

"Fairly expensive, I thought," she said "but I really want it."

"Um," said Frank.

"Actually it was quite expensive, darling, it was over four hundred dollars."

"What!" Frank lifted his head and looked at her, astonished. After the money for the tiles and the couch and the tables and the pots and the shrubs, he couldn't believe this. Has she gone mad? Was he made of money? Good God, they only had the pension.

"Four hundred dollars!" He shouted at her. "Are you bonkers? Where do you think we"re going to get that sort of money. You stupid bloody cow."

Monica froze. Stupid cow. Her mother's words, used over and over again. Stupid cow. Stupid cow.

"I've had enough of this madness." Frank got up from the table. " This has got to stop. I'm going to bed." Slamming the passage door behind him, he left.

Monica sat perfectly still at her table, her hands on her lap. She sat there for several hours, unmoving, the uncleared dishes cluttering the table before her.

Eventually she rose and quietly opening the passage door went to the bedroom where Frank lay on his back snoring in the bed. She stood and looked at him for a while, her face unmoving, then turned and left the room. She went into the laundry where she picked up the torch, turned it on and went out the back to Frank's shed where she found the hammer.

Without a falter in her steps, she returned to the bedroom, turned the hammer on its side and, swinging her arm outwards to give her leverage, she slammed the side of the hammer head against Frank's temple. She was a strong woman. It only took one blow.

WHILE she had been sitting at the table Monica had worked out how she could pay for the red dress.

The old-age pensions for the two of them were paid directly into their joint account. They both accessed the money using their bank cards and PIN numbers at the machines. If for any reason there was a necessity to deal directly with a teller in the bank itself, Monica had always been the one to handle it when shopping. She knew Frank's PIN number. They had worked them out together and she had, in fact, already once used his card when she'd misplaced her purse.

As well as that they had both signed over their power

of attorney to each other when Frank retired. The account-
ant who organised the superannuation and house pay-
ment had insisted on it when he did their wills. She should
be well covered at the bank.

There would still be two pensions coming in and only
her own personal expenses to be met. There was enough
money left in their savings to pay for the red dress with a
little to spare, so she'd be right.

Frank, she surmised, would probably not even be
missed. What a dreadful thought. Sad. How many other
people who lived insular lives could live and die without
anybody really noticing? There must be thousands, mused
Monica, surprised at her own sudden insight. Well now,
there's a thought! A television program popped into her
head, a police show of some sort about a homeless man
who was murdered and their inability to find out who he
was or what sort of life he had lived. It was as if he had
never existed. At the time it had caused a twinge of panic
somewhere deep inside her, which was why she had remembered it, but only now did that panic threaten to surface. Each so alone. What if she slipped and fell? Would
she ever be found? What would it matter to the rest of the
world? Of course, she reasoned quickly, the bills would
not be paid and the bank would notice lack of activity
eventually. Grabbing hold of this sane thought, back to the
safety of reality, she retreated back into her usual narrow
limit of thought.

Of late, since the verandah, she had often surprised
herself with a foreign, vague exploration of possibility.
She didn't understand where these images came from and
wore them uneasily. Still, they had led her to the verandah
and an excitement she'd never experienced before.

Pulling herself together, she thought she had better deal
with Frank and, in her usual thorough manner, sat down
at the table with a pen and writing pad to make a list.

The body. She'd deal with that last as it would take
some time to work it out. The bank. She drew a line

straight through that one. Family. He only had one living brother, married, who still lived in England. She was the one who wrote all of the letters, Frank was not much of a writer, and she could continue to do so. Easy. She drew a line through that one. Friends. Well, there never had been many and everyone retired now and living in different suburbs. If, by chance, anybody rang or visited she could always say Frank had a short-term cash job in the country. Nobody had called, to her knowledge, for the last two years anyway, so she drew a line through that one.

Oh, the pub. The only place he ever went on a semi-regular basis. Not really a concern she figured. He'd never mentioned anybody by name from the pub, only "this chap" or "that chap". They'd probably miss his betting money on the TAB, she smiled grimly, but that lot was going into her purse from now on.

The neighbours. That could be a slight problem. Not enough to worry about really she thought. Whenever either of them had gone out they'd been in the car, alone or together. Sometimes Frank used the trailer, not often. She'd leave that where it was, at the rear of the garage. Frank kept himself to himself and as far as she knew, since they'd finished the front garden and had given a cursory nod to a car driving by now and then Frank hadn't had anything to do lately with any of the neighbours. Except, she remembered suddenly, the owner of the verandah. He'd spoken to her about the fence and then she supposed there may have been some contact while it was being built. None though that she could remember him mentioning. That'd be okay.

The Nelsons, on the other side, lived at such a pace with the three children, always in and out in the car. No, she thought, they'd never notice. When their houses were finished they had introduced themselves to each other as they worked in their front yards, and there was that one barbecue years ago, but the young couple obviously had no interest in the two retirees. They lived a different life with many interests, none of which could possibly involve two withdrawn oldies. A couple of times, over the years, one of the kids would arrive at the door selling raffle tickets or biscuits for the school. Monica always bought something and could see no reason why she still couldn't. She could even, she dared to think, call out "Frank, have you got my purse," in earshot of the child. What a thought. How clever she was getting.

They had never officially met the owners of the houses across the wide road. They had seen them, of course, backing their cars out and heard the excited yells of their children as they tore up and down the street on whatever was the latest fad, but there was no contact with them at all.

She ran a line through neighbours.

Now everything was dealt with except the body and, as she made herself a cup of tea, she pondered the best way to deal with that.

She wasn't smart or devious by nature like the characters she saw on the television crime shows. She didn't really know very much at all except what she'd learnt at the nursery and then the skills of home-making. For a moment she considered burying Frank in the back yard but quickly dismissed the idea. She could never dig a hole big enough and it would be just her luck that some kid's ball would come over the fence and she'd be caught. And the lifting? She was not a young woman anymore, though strong for her age. Then she thought of the compost heap. Could there be a way? Blood and bone, blood and bone.

The cup of tea became cold in front of her as she sat. She had pins and needles in her feet by the time she'd decided on a plan. Well a sort of plan. She'd have to see how she went.

Pieces, she thought, pieces.

Manageable.

Small pieces into some sort of acid, then buried.

A wave of horror passed over her. What had she done? What was she thinking? Then it passed, as quickly as it had come, and she thought of the red dress. No turning back now, anyway.

She moved to the sliding door of the dinette and stood there a moment, looking out at her white couch on the tiles, then, moving slowly over to the freezer, she lifted the lid and looked inside. Quite a lot of room in there if she took out the ice cream and ate some of the meat, packaged neatly into portions for two. That freezer was jolly handy when Pete was a growing lad and why they'd bothered to keep it just for the two of them she'd no idea. But there it was, practically empty.

Common sense told her she'd better start soon. Whatever it was that she was going to do. Somehow Frank had to move from the bed to the freezer to the acid. Just how wasn't clear. She'd need some help. She'd need tools.

Monica went out to Frank's shed. She shut the door behind her and switched on the lights. She stood, carefully observing every facet of the set-up Frank had arranged to make his precious horses. She'd never really looked at the shed's interior closely. She came in every week to get Frank's overalls and left. She was surprised at how many tools there were in the shed, and the variety. After standing a few moments or so, motionless, planning, she returned to the house with a large sheet of strong plastic that she'd spied folded on a shelf, and a hacksaw, and took them into the bedroom.

Frank lay still under the covers. There was a bit of blood on the pillow and the top of one of the blankets, but not much. She pulled the blankets off and dropped them on the floor, Frank lay there still and defenceless. He was only wearing underpants. She put her hand on his chest. He was cold. She picked up one arm and dropped it so it thumped on to the bed.

Not stiff yet, she thought, thankfully. That would have made everything much harder. She spread the black plastic on the floor beside the bed then, leaning, she rolled Frank over towards her so that he lay face down right on the edge of the mattress. Whew, harder than she'd have imagined; he was heavy. She took a step back and with her hands on her hips, breathing deeply, she surveyed the scene. She would have to heave him right off the bed so that he'd fall on the plastic. She pushed the edge of the plastic further under the bed with her foot, then, everything in place, she grabbed him by the far side of his underpants and his far shoulder and pulled as hard as she could, swinging him over and down in one movement. She had to jump back quickly so that he didn't fall on her feet and was shocked by the heavy thump that he made when he hit the floor.

For a moment Monica sat down on the chair in the corner of the bedroom where Frank had thrown his clothes. She looked along the passage to the bathroom door trying to judge how much effort it would take to get him there. She had already dismissed the small en-suite that joined on to the bedroom. Not anywhere near enough room in there with just the shower and the toilet. The second bathroom, with a bath, was far roomier, but farther to go. She stood up, took a deep, determined breath, grabbed hold of the end of the plastic nearest the door and pulled as hard as she could, backing out of the bedroom along the passage. With an almighty effort she got him to the bathroom door in one go. She straightened and leaned against the door frame breathing heavily. For an old boy he certainly weighed a lot.

Oh, she needed a cuppa.

Sitting at the end of the table where she could look along the hallway Monica sipped her coffee. The moral problem of murder never entered her head. The problem, as she saw it, was how to get him into the bath. If she faltered, she knew, she'd never find the strength again so, finishing her coffee quickly, she nearly ran down the passage, grabbed hold of the plastic again and with two good tugs got Frank alongside the bath. Then, drawing a deep breath, grabbing his underarms she heaved Frank's torso over the edge of the bath. She was surprised at her own strength; adrenalin running high. Legs and feet were easy after that and with another thump he was in.

She made sure the plug hole was free, then choosing the sharpest knife from the kitchen she neatly sliced down both wrists and ankles and then across Frank's stomach and throat, dispassionately watching the blood ooze slowly out. Satisfied and pleased with her accomplishment she shut the bathroom door behind her and left him to bleed.

Monica had seen on the tele how they gutted and hung the meat on farms. Tomorrow she would have to tackle the gutting, but for now she was content. Exhausted, she fell asleep on the vinyl lounge in front of the tele.

Monica awoke, stiff and cold, in the early hours of the morning. The television still blaring. She wrapped her arms about herself, shivering, and sat rocking back and forth on the seat for a while. Remembering.

She had no choice now. There was no going back. She must finish the job.

Switching on the small electric heater in the kitchen, she made herself some toast and tea. Thinking, thinking all the while; the easiest way, the quickest way, the safest way.

Well into autumn now, the nights were beginning to get cold but the days were often warm, too warm to leave the body unattended for too long. With a shudder she remembered the next job. Gutting the corpse. She'd gutted many fish in her time and a few rabbits back in the days when Frank and Peter went shooting. Not her favourite job, but manageable.

Peter. Suddenly she remembered his books, packed away somewhere in one of the boxes in one of the spare bedrooms. Just why they'd kept all of Pete's stuff she didn't know. Somehow it seemed wrong to throw everything out. She was sure she remembered some biology books among the pile. Could prove to be handy. She'd have a look later.

But now. Now she must get started on the worst job. It was not yet 5a.m. Grimly putting on her extra-length rubber gloves, she collected a dozen or so plastic bags and the knife block and resolutely went into the bathroom. She was still wearing yesterday's dress and cardigan, but they could go into the rubbish. She remembered that she'd have the money to buy new clothes now and the thought lifted her sagging spirit, making the chore ahead of her a fraction easier.

Nearly two hours later she came out of the bathroom with three plastic bags, hanging heavy with their contents. A pile more were stacked beside the bath, ready to be sealed and put in the freezer. All were tagged tightly, put inside second bags which were also sealed tightly and then stacked neatly along one side of the freezer. She shut the lid firmly and put the kettle on. She needed a coffee and a sit-down. Her back was aching and her knees hurt. She put two painkillers in a glass of water and sat watching vacantly as they slowly dissolved.

Water, she thought. She'd need a lot of water. Tiredly getting up, she drank the painkillers and filled a bucket of water at the sink. She trudged slowly along the passage, weary now, then returned for a second refill. One more for now, she decided, then she would clean the room properly after the job was completely finished. She'd like to be done by lunchtime, she thought. Then a bit of shopping and a good lie-down. Lie down. The blanket and pillowcase popped into her head. She collected them both, and the sheets and put them into the washing machine. They could go to St Vincent de Paul's, she decided. If they went straight into the drier she could take them today.

Pleased with herself, she made a bacon and egg sandwich and ate it with relish. She realised she had forgotten to finish her meal the night before and was quite hungry. When she went to the mall, she decided, she'd pop in and buy a nice quiche from the bakery.

Meals, she suddenly realised, would cease to be a problem anymore. She only had herself to think of.

A bonus.

Rested and refreshed, she thought about tackling the next problem with Frank. She remembered cutting through the joints of a chicken to section it for casseroles and wondered if the whole job could be that simple.

Feeling hopeful that her task might be easier than expected, she began looking through the boxes of Peter's stuff where she eventually found his books. She had to leaf through several before she found what she was looking for, a picture of the human skeleton. She took the book into the bathroom and propped it open at the appropriate page in the sink.

Once again donning her rubber gloves (what a good buy they had been, she chuckled) and taking her newest titanium knife set to supplement the others and the hacksaw, she returned to the bathroom where she cut, chopped and sawed until the job was done.

Good thing she recently bought a jumbo pack of garbage bags, she thought. Better restock those next visit to the shops.

The green garbage bags, too, were taken to the bathroom and one by one they came out with half a limb, or other body part wrapped inside and were deposited in the freezer until the bath was empty except for a few small bone chips and a bit of mess. Expertly she scooped these up and popped them into a smaller plastic bag and into the garbage.

She stood for a few moments in the bathroom doorway, surveying the room. It would require a thorough clean, she knew, but not today. Her aching back was nearly unbearable and she'd cut one of her fingers when a knife slipped. She was tired and sore. Tomorrow. Tomorrow she'd tackle the bathroom.

Stripping her soiled clothing off, she left it in a pile on the floor and showered in the en-suite. She looked at herself in the mirror, old and naked. She still looked the same as she had this time yesterday. Smiling at her reflection she wondered what else she'd expected.

Feeling clean and fresh she put on her best underwear and her dressing gown. She was surprised to find that it was already nearly two o'clock and lay on the couch in front of the tele for a snooze before preparing for the afternoon on the verandah. No time for the mall today.

Rested, at three, Monica surveyed her sorry collection of clothes. It was quite cold she realised, chilly from lying on the couch without the heater on, and there was not much choice to wear today. Her one thick black skirt would have to do and her only tidy jumper which was dark blue. Very plain, she thought, surveying the result, and no scarf to wear with it. Oh well, it wouldn't be long before she could buy some new things and with this cheering knowledge she decided stubbornly that she didn't care so much today what appeared on the other verandah. Things would change.

Nevertheless, when she stepped out at 3.30 she still felt a little thrill of pleasure to see a black skirt at least. Raising her glass to the soft aqua jumper with a loose roll neck, noting every detail so that she could find one the same, Monica felt good. Sipping her wine she found that she enjoyed the warm hit of alcohol in her stomach for the first time and she happily continued her love story until it was time to go inside.

Once she was back in the house however she realised how tired she was, her back still sore and her shoulders stiff from the day's work and sitting reading for so long. Skipping tea, she went to the bedroom and made up the bed with clean sheets and pillowcases as well as the doona from the spare room. Frank didn't like doonas, he liked blankets. Well, she could choose now, and with the bed clean and empty she striped off and slipped naked between the sheets where she stretched comfortably across the mattress and slept like a baby.

V

Frank

FRANK knocked tentatively on the front door of the two-storey house next door. Why he had to do this was beyond him. Why couldn't Mon have asked her? The whole business was stupid as far as he could see. Still, life had certainly been much more pleasurable since Mon had begun that whole silly verandah idea. Extra special meals, not to mention the sex.

He knocked again, then noticed the bell-push on the door frame. He pushed. Chimes rang loudly inside the house and within moments Miss Trante opened the door.

"Yes?" she inquired sternly.

"Er, I'm Frank from next door. I'm here about the fence."

"What fence?" The woman asked sharply. What on earth could this old fellow be on about?

"Well, our fence," he said, wishing he hadn't come. "My wife has an idea ..."

"Well, yes?"

Hesitantly Frank tried to explain. His wife had thought of extending the low brick wall further along between the houses. To the edge of the back verandahs, in fact. And pull down the iron one. He was a builder, he explained, and would do the job himself at no cost to her.

Well, how very odd, thought Miss Trante. These people had never spoken to her in the four or so years since they'd moved in. Mind you, she hadn't approached them either. She kept herself to herself and they didn't look like the sort of people she'd associate with anyway. She'd seen

them out in the front garden when they first moved in. A plain couple, with no imagination, she'd thought, watching them plant their front yard to match all the others. Not her type at all.

The neighbour in overalls (overalls, for goodness sake) was standing awkwardly waiting for an answer.

"No cost to me, you say?" She inquired.

"None whatever, lady. I'll supply the bricks and do the labour myself. I've got plenty of experience and I'll do a good job."

"Well, let me think about it," said Miss Trante. "Come back the day after tomorrow, between noon and three, and I'll let you know."

"Ok," said Frank and, dismissed by the abrupt closure of the door, stomped back home to Mon.

Miss Trante, Janine, returned to her chair and her book, but after reading only one paragraph she lowered the book to her lap.

What an extraordinary request, she thought. What possible reason could they have to extend the low brick wall? She herself loathed the iron fencing. It was so tacky. The one thing about her home that she was unhappy with.

When she bought the house, the estate was still mostly all paddocks. The eight display homes were mostly at the entrance to the new area, but her own and the other larger two-storey home for some reason had been placed further back and on separate streets. She had queried the choice of the iron fence at the time and the agent, pointing out that this was standard throughout the estate, told her that once she had neighbouring homes she could negotiate with the owners to change the fence, each owner paying half by law. The thought of dealing with these people, one each side, had been too much and to date she had let it slip.

But this, this extension of the low brick fence, was slightly weird. There must be a reason for it. She had seen, from her own verandah where she liked to sit with a glass of wine and a book in the late afternoons, the roof of the neighbouring verandah. It had looked, from where she sat, as if it extended the full length of the house. Recently though, she'd become aware of brickwork blocking part of it off. She'd paid very little attention to it but decided she should have a look over the fence to see exactly what was going on. She certainly didn't want her privacy invaded by an eyesore. Of course, if it came to it, she could always plant a couple more shrubs. There would be room for them if the iron fence went.

Miss Trante was reasonably tall, but not tall enough to see over the two-metre fence. She lifted the chair from under the small table and after removing the velvet cushion stood on it to have a quick peek at the neighbour's yard. She desperately hoped nobody would see her. How embarrassing. But no-one was in sight.

What she saw, however, gave her quite a shock. There before her was a mirror image of her own verandah. Table, couch, tiles, plants, the lot. She stepped off the chair quickly and sat on it for a moment, stunned. How could this be? It had taken her months to decide on the decor for her verandah. She couldn't believe that by chance that woman next door... No, Of course not. Well, what then?

Creeping up for another look Miss Trante's eyes swung around the garden. Shrubs, the same shrubs as her own had been planted in a curve symmetrical to her own with a newly planted lawn fighting its way to greenness between the garden and the verandah. Even the trees, not tall enough yet for her to have seen them over the height of the fence had been planted to mimic her own.

Replacing the chair and cushion in their proper places she went inside and poured herself a stiff whisky. Dumbfounded, she sat at the dining room table, looking out upon her own verandah and sipped the drink.

Her first and immediate reaction was that of horror. This bizarre occurrence must be undone. She would not have it.

She had a screaming urge to have another look but controlled it. She knew what she had seen. That woman, that slob of a woman next door had COPIED her verandah.

What a cheek.

What a nerve.

AND her garden. Her shrubs.

Beyond belief or understanding she poured herself a second whisky. Why, for God's sake would anybody ever do that? She well knew, for she was a well-educated woman of the world, that imitation was the highest form of flattery. But a verandah?

That afternoon Miss Trante skipped her daily sojourn on her back verandah. She sat at her Italian antique dining table and drank half a bottle of very good quality whisky. She had experienced many and varied weird experiences on her travels overseas during school holidays, but none of them were on her own home turf, her safe ground and she was shocked to the core.

It took quite a lot to shock Miss Trante. She had run a school for girls and had dealt with difficult children, teachers and parents for many years. Retired for five years now, just gone seventy, she had bought this particular house instead of a smart unit in the city because her love was travel and the majority of her superannuation and savings had been ear-marked for this pleasure, much of it already gone. She also needed quite a bit of room for her antiques and treasures collected through a lifetime of journeys overseas, all now beautifully displayed as they should be.

She was an extremely solitary woman. Over the years she'd accustomed herself to this loneliness by surrounding herself with music, books and things of beauty.

She had come to Australia from London with her mother when she was in her early teens, the move brought about by the involvement of her father, who she adored, with a black magic cult at the small university where he was a professor of literature. Her well-bred snobbish mother had not been able to handle the scandal and had chosen to settle in Victoria, Australia, where she had relatives who could be relied upon until she could get settled.

Mother had been born into money and was well-educated and attractive. She was also extremely self-centred and had never really taken to her plain, gangly daughter who had been raised by a nanny until she was old enough to go to school. Once mother had established herself in a smart, rented townhouse in the city of Melbourne and had organised invitations to the plethora of functions of the Victorian social set, there was no room in her life for her daughter whom she saw as an embarrassment and she packed her off to a reputable boarding school.

Janine Trante did not like boarding school but found it preferable to living with mother who always managed to find some fault with her looks, her manner or her behaviour. She had grown into a tall, studious girl with thinnish brown hair and a sharpish nose, quiet and private to the extreme and did not fit in with the buxom, blossoming beauties of her class who ran with a young social set full of snobbish pretensions. She missed her father dreadfully and they exchanged long letters which were her only joy other than her studies where she excelled in French and her beloved English.

During holiday breaks mother sent her overseas to stay with her father and her love of travel stemmed from these precious breaks away to whichever spot on the planet in which he happened to be working. Father, though he loved her and always welcomed her with warmth and joy, made it plain that his daily world had no room for her. He had become a sort of wandering tutor, taking contract teaching jobs in any country that he fancied and his nomad life was not suitable for a child completing the standard of education that he wished for her. Their holidays, however, opened up a world of exploration and pleasure that became Janine Trante's passion and reason for living.

At boarding school Janine excelled at her study and on finishing her courses there she moved on to university and then teaching. Although her demeanour was quiet she was aggressively ambitious and soon climbed the ladder to senior mistress and then head mistress.

While studying at university she moved back with mother, who was hardly home anyway, and slowly the two women gradually adapted to each other's idiosyncrasies and stayed together in the large townhouse until mother died. She died bitter and broke having squandered a fortune on the good life, unattached and disillusioned. Janine, Miss Trante by now (with an "e") found herself unable to grieve for mother at all and soon began to enjoy her solitude, happily alone with no one to answer to.

Her life revolved around beautiful possessions, books, travel, fine wine and good food. She had been content enough; a solitary unit.

And now this.

Miss Trante had never been the envy of anybody. Not ever. Certainly she had been admired and respected for her scholastic abilities, her fluent French and her positions of authority. She had been held in awe and often feared. She had been disliked too by many of her peers being an unknown quantity, always on the defensive. Touchy, edgy and manipulative, she had not been an easy woman to befriend.

Her mother's outgoing personality had not been passed down to her. She had inherited, though, much of her father's introspection and love of the unusual, neither of which had endeared her to the rest of the girls at the boarding school. Their interests, mostly boys, clothes, money and a good time all seemed of little value to her and she easily became withdrawn behind the safety of books, even back then, a place where nothing was expected of her but passive participation.

Vicariously, though, she had learnt a bit about presentation, and her taste in clothes was smart and her appearance well-kept. Not that she could do much with a tall, thin body and a long face with the sharp nose already confronting before she herself was. Her mother had also encouraged her to dress well, in tailored suits of subdued colour. And she found, over the years, especially when travelling, that quiet and dark colours kept one unnoticed in a crowd. Sometimes she yearned for colour and life but other than an occasional pale floral blouse she didn't have the courage or persona to carry them off.

Only recently, she thought, sipping the last of her whisky, had she broken out and bought that dress. Her mind flashed up to the bedroom where it hung on its hanger over the top of the door, visible from her bed. What would mother have said? And at her age! But there it hung, not yet worn, a splash of bright red in the subdued hue of the bedroom furnishings.

Placing the empty glass on a coaster her thoughts returned to the surprising visit of the afternoon.

I wish Daddy was still alive, she thought wistfully. She and her father had shared an excitement, an expectation of the unknown, which they'd satisfied with travel, visiting lesser known areas, venturing down unmarked roads.

Since her father's passing from a stroke, some 20 years back, she'd travelled alone and had generally continued the pattern, steering away from tourist destinations.

Once, sick of always being by herself with no-one to share the excitement, she'd booked into a safari group in Africa.

The trip itself had been quite rewarding but living in close proximity to a dozen others, mostly young, had been unpleasant and distasteful. With all of the people skills she had needed for her job, she still found communication with the rest of the group quite difficult and before the tour was halfway through she promised herself that she would never do it again.

She was used to pleasing herself, first and foremost, and singular travel was the best way. In this manner she could choose to stop at a favourite village for as long as she wished, exploring the roads and examining the home-made crafts to her hearts content, ever alert for that one special piece. Expecting the unknown at every turn she made.

This verandah situation is an unknown, she thought. What would Daddy have advised? Instantly she knew exactly what Daddy would have said. Explore the possibility. But she was not so convinced. This was not a town or a country she could easily leave behind. This was her territory, her home.

The thought of maybe having to leave her nice little set-up was horrific. She had spent a lot of time arranging the interior of her house, filled with the precious antiques and the beautiful objects she had collected from all over the world. At any time she could pick up a pot or stroke a sculpture and be transported instantly back to the smells, the temperature and the mystic of its homeland.

Her last trip, including America and even New York, an adventure for any lone traveller, had nearly wiped out the last of her travel money. Having paid for the house outright from her generous super, she blew the rest on a world trip reasoning at her age that she may not be physically capable for much longer. And she would never, never be part of the elderly groups that took guided tours and spent the majority of their holiday in buses and smart hotels, each city indistinguishable one from the other.

So she was stuck now, certainly stuck comfortably, but stuck nevertheless. Could she possibly sell-up and move somewhere else if things became unbearable, she questioned. But no, glancing around her lounge room at her treasures she decided she couldn't do it all again. The move from mother's house to this one had been horrendous, the worry of a piece being damaged by the careless moving contractors had nearly killed her.

Well, what then?

Tired of thinking about this sudden problem dropped in her lap, she reached for the new book lying on the sideboard.

Miss Trante only read good books. She did not believe

in newspapers or magazines except for an occasional *Australian Vogue* to check the fashions. Books were her love, each one of those an unknown until it was open. An escape from time, too, time the enemy sometimes when living a solitary life. But she could not read for long, tired from whisky and thought, and soon took herself upstairs to bed. Tomorrow, she thought, tomorrow is another day.

The next morning she awoke aware of a vague sense of excitement. Then she remembered, the back verandah. Curbing her desire to go and have another look immediately, she prepared her muesli and fruit and sat at the table to eat. This morning, passing by the radio absently, she didn't flick it on the ABC for her usual program. She was halfway through the bowl before she became aware of the silence.

Well, she thought, surprised, this verandah business must be getting to me. She had to look. Leaving her breakfast unfinished and still in her dressing gown she went outside and listened at the fence for any sounds of activity. Without removing the velvet cushion, for she had soft slippers on, she quietly moved the chair to the fence and stood on it. Suddenly aware of what she was doing she glanced along the narrow space dividing the two houses where she could be visible from the street. Thankfully there was nobody to be seen. She never went outside in her gown and a picture of herself so attired, standing on a chair, peering over the fence popped into her head. Her tight, thin lips formed a smile and she nearly blushed with embarrassment.

Still, she was here, so she might as well have a look. She peered cautiously over the fence. Yes it was all still there, she hadn't dreamed it.

There was nobody around and she took a closer note of the scene than she had done the previous day. The tiles, she observed, were not unlike her own at first glance. The blue pattern, the right colour at least, was very similar in design but the tiles were obviously a cheap copy of her own which had come from Italy. The glass tables and matching chair were identical. With some satisfaction she noted that the couch was quite different. Certainly a white leather two-seater but not anywhere near the quality of hers. Miss Trante had an eye for furniture and could tell the difference immediately. It lacked that essence of style on which she prided herself and the leather was of much inferior quality. Not anywhere near as comfortable she knew, but there it sat anyway, a poor attempt at a replica of her own.

The pot plants, however, were a surprise. The large blue pots were identical and the plants themselves looked healthy and strong. She swung her eyes to the shrubs, obviously planted long after her own, and noted that they were in fine condition, flowering more plentifully than hers. This person, she acknowledged, must be good with plants.

After another quick glance at the astonishing scene she stepped down, replaced the chair and went inside. Taking her unfinished muesli to the sink she returned to the dining room where she poured herself a whisky, put on a Brahm's CD and sat in contemplation until the music finished.

What had she to lose, she thought. She was already caught in the web of anticipation that made her feel alive. She hadn't felt this way since New York. And here she was having a whisky before lunch. Unheard of. With a touch of scorn, perhaps tinged with pity, she thought of the pottery piece on next door's glass table. A tawdry piece, lacking in style and quality, quite unlike her own which was one of a pair she'd bought in Mexico, delicate and beautiful to the touch.

Whatever might eventuate (the thought made her breathless) she would obviously have to be the winner. Yes, she decided, she would let that old man pull down the fence. She felt elated, in control.

Hungry, now that the decision had been made, she

cooked herself an omelette, light and fluffy, generously filled with cheese and herbs and ate it with pleasure.

VI

Monica's couch

TWO days after Frank had finished the verandah wall, Monica noticed an ad in the local monthly paper which she always read religiously from front to back. This was where you found the sales and with their limited income was a good resource for important purchases. Not that they ever bought anything much, she thought, since neither of them were very materialistic and their needs were small. Frank sometimes might buy a new tool or a ladder at the sales or they'd get something small for the kitchen. Their savings were limited and precious and Monica, who handled all the finances, was a canny shopper and careful with every cent. They would be able to manage quite well on their pensions, the car paid off and the house free of finance, except for Frank's gambling and beer. Not that Monica begrudged him this if he could keep it to a stable amount, but often, chasing a win on the pokies or the horses, he'd spend too much and the house-keeping money would have to suffer.

The ad that caught Monica's eye was for the tile shop in the shopping mall. She'd never been in there before, having no reason, but thought that while she was out, she'd pop in and see what they had, the blue and white tiles from next door's verandah at the back of her mind. As it happened there were some blue and white tiles on special. Monica tried to remember exactly what the ones next door had looked like. About the same colour blue, she thought, but the pattern had simply looked a bit squiggly.

"Can I have tile to take?," she asked, amazed at her audacity. "I'll bring it back tomorrow, but must check that it's the right one."

"Of course," said the assistant "and measurements please, we only have a few of those left."

Panicking a little, Monica rushed home with the tile. It was nearly lunch time and she hoped Frank would still be in the shed. He usually stayed there until she called him. She didn't want him to see her with the tile yet.

Hoping, hoping, hoping there was nobody about next door, she furtively got the box and cautiously looked over the fence. Good, nobody there. She had the tile in one hand and compared it with those on the verandah floor. The pattern was slightly different, she could see when looking carefully, but the colour blue was pretty damned close and the amount of blue and white on the tile was very similar. A blue edge though. She thought she mightn't find much better, especially on sale at nearly half-price. She hopped down quickly, having decided already, and looked at her verandah. How could she measure it without getting Frank's tape from the shed and giving the game away. The thought horrified her.

Getting pencil and paper from the kitchen she paced out the verandah, one foot before the other and with these measurements in hand she drove straight back to the tile shop. The assistant had no trouble converting her measurements to a usable scale and working out a price for the required amount of tiles. And, yes, they had a matching border tile, not on special though.

"That's all right," said Monica, "I'll have them. I'll just pop up to the machine and get the money, while you pack them up. Could you carry them to my car, do you think?"

Assured of the tiles as hers, Monica took out a bit extra for a nice piece of rump steak for Frank's tea. She mentioned nothing about the purchase at lunch, but when Frank returned from the pub that evening, mellow with beer and savouring his delicious steak, she began.

" I'm so pleased with that wall, Frank. You did such a wonderful job. It will make all the difference if we want to sit out there. I've been thinking that I'd like to make it really pretty."

"Um," said Frank, barely listening.

"As a matter of fact," Monica continued "I saw some nice tiles at the shop today that would go nice on the floor."

"Um," said Frank.

"There was a big sale on," she continued "and they were really cheap so I bought some."

"What!" Frank looked up from his dinner in astonishment.

"They were really cheap, Frank, and I thought I could stick them down myself. It won't mean any work for you."

She smiled at him coyly. "You need your strength for other things, don't you darling?" She said suggestivly.

"Tiles," said Frank, still stunned. "You bought tiles."

In all their years together Monica had never shown any interest in decorating of any sort, Never. Even when they'd built the new house she'd left the choice of bathroom and kitchen tiles up to him. "That's your field," she'd said. "You know best." And now this! He couldn't believe it.

"It will make a nice area," Monica was saying. "In the summer we could even eat out there sometimes. It could be quite romantic." She moved around the table to remove his dinner plate and replace it with sweets, his favourite steamed pudding. Bending down she kissed him softly on the cheek.

"What do you think?" She ventured, "Won't it look nice?"

Frank didn't know what to think. Tiles, for Christ's sake. And lay them herself. Fat chance. Now that'd be a real waste of money. What the hell's got into the woman? But on a promise, already kissed on the cheek, and seeing her so set on it, he gave in. They were already bought, anyway, and on sale, he knew, not returnable.

"Well I suppose I could lay them a hell of a lot quicker than you," he said and was rewarded with a beaming smile.

"Oh, would you? What a sweetheart your are. Shall we have coffee and an early night do you think? I'll just do these dishes while you watch a bit of tele then we'll go to bed, eh?"

"Suits me," said Frank, hardly believing his luck. Again. Well, if she was going through some sort of hormone thing, he might as well enjoy it. What's a few tiles here and there. Probably would look nice anyway.

So the tiles were soon down and Monica's search for furniture began. A glass-topped round table, with a matching chair quietly put on lay-by. Easier to find than she imagined, once she was actually looking. No small table was available, but one ordered, to match the bigger one. The couch was more difficult, all of those at the mall too expensive and Monica daren't spend too much.

One night, watching the tele with Frank, her eye was caught with a picture of a white two-seater on sale in some warehouse in the city. Very cheap.

"Oh, Frank," she breathed excitedly, "wouldn't that be nice on the verandah."

"S'pose," mumbled Frank, hoping this was not going to be yet another expense. "Leather, though Mon. We don"t need leather. The other stuff's vinyl and that's okay."

"Yes, but outside, in case of weather, it would last much longer," she suggested.

Last longer, thought Frank. Christ it'd outlast us. Woman's bloody mad. But looking over at her, her old face glowing with a youthful excitement, he softened. Poor old girl. She'd never really asked for much. And she'd been so loving lately. Maybe they could just manage it, if it was as cheap as the ad suggested.

"Anyway, darling, I need you to come with me to that big nursery to collect the plants for the back garden. They're too big for me to handle and we'll need the trailer. We could make a day of it and have a nice lunch somewhere. Perhaps look at some tools for you while we're in the city."

Tools, thought Frank hopefully for a second, I'd like a band saw. It'd make the horses a hell of a lot easier. But the way the old girl was spending money he doubted there'd be enough for a pair of pliers. They only had a few thousand put by. Still, he wouldn't mind checking out those saws. You never know.

"All right, Mon, we'll have a look. But it all depends on the price."

"Tomorrow," she said, "let's go tomorrow."

"Maybe," he answered, unwilling to commit immediately, but after she took his hand and led him to the bedroom, after she did things for him that she'd never done before, he was happy enough to set out for town the next day.

"Tool shop first," said Monica on the way to the city "then lunch, then we'll take a look at those couches. Nursery on the way home."

"Um," said Frank, but secretly pleased that she was putting his wants before her own. He wouldn't mind having a look around that new tool complex. Could pick up a bargain. And they did. A fabulous band-saw bigger and stronger than the one he already had which had given him a hell of a lot of trouble when he was cutting the heads for his rocking horses. At a pinch he could have managed without this new beauty, but boy's toys are boy's toys and this big machine at such a low price was just too good to pass up. And Mon had been wonderful. She hadn't blinked an eye at the $750 price tag. He was worth it, she had said, nudging him gently in the ribs. He couldn't wait to get it home and try it out.

"Cut through anything, this," he said proudly as he loaded it on the trailer. "What a beauty." Feeling young and vital again, a man with a new saw, he took his wife to an Italian restaurant for lunch, with a table by the window so he could keep a sharp eye on the trailer.

"Have a beer, darling," said Mon, ordering a spring water. "I can drive if necessary as long as you back the trailer in at home."

"C'mon, Mon," he answered, "I can have a couple and still drive okay. You just relax and be waited on for a change." The man. The man with a new saw. He felt good. And what a lovely meal they had; pasta entree and veal scaloppine for mains. Washed down with a couple of imported beers. Frank was a happy man.

They drove to the leather warehouse where they were both astounded by the dozens and dozens of suites on display. And at reasonably good prices, they thought. Not many white ones though, and those mainly three-seaters with matching chairs. "We saw a white two-seater on the television?" Monica queried an attendant. "We don't want a whole suite."

"Oh yeah. Only a couple of those left. Down the end of that aisle."

And there they were. Slightly marked but nothing Monica couldn't clean up. She sat down on one and patted the seat next to her for Frank. "Quite comfy, isn't it?" she asked him. "And what a good price. Marked down to half according to the ticket. Only six hundred and ninety-nine dollars."

"Um," said Frank, mellowed with food and beer and thinking about his new saw.

"Oh, Frank, I really love it. We could take it with us now in the trailer and get the plants tomorrow," breathed Monica excitedly. "What do you think?"

"Well . . ." tried Frank.

"But there's only two left. If we don't get it now someone else will buy them. At this price."

"All right Mon," said Frank feeling magnanimous. "You pay for it and find someone to give us a hand. I'll back the trailer up."

And so it was. Monica had her couch and Frank had his saw. The two of them drove home in happy silence, each dreaming their own dream, content with life and each other.

The following day Frank didn't want to drive to the nursery and pick up the plants that Monica had ordered and paid for. He spent the whole day in the shed playing with his new saw. That was fine for Monica who, sitting on her new white couch on the back verandah, spent the whole day planning exactly where which plant would go. Every now and then she'd hop up on the box and check over the fence to see exactly how they should be placed and then she'd get a stone and place it to mark where each hole should go.

At half-past three, just as she was about to climb on the box again, she heard a sound from next door's verandah. She froze. Another second or two and she would have been caught peering over the fence. Carefully and quietly she moved away from the fence and went inside to check the time. She would be sure to listen the next day and the day after to see if the verandah was always occupied at the same time. She sat on the white couch for a while surveying the back yard and planning in her head, then went inside to begin Frank's roast. She wanted to thank him for her white couch and guarantee his willingness to make the trip to the nursery the next day.

Early next morning (nice and early, Frank, so as not to disturb your work in the shed) they collected the plants in the trailer. Well-established shrubs, quite high and some flowering, and a couple of two-metre high lemon-scented gums. Frank carried them all to their allocated spots, but Monica assured him that she would dig the holes and plant them herself. It took her all morning and well into the afternoon, working solidly, to get them all settled into their new environment. Monica had a way with plants and her careful preparation of each hole guaranteed their easy adaptation. She watered them in carefully, keeping an eye on her watch, until just after three o'clock.

Tired but satisfied with her day's work, she made two

coffees, took one out to Frank in the shed with a piece of fruitcake, then sat with her own on the couch on the verandah, listening carefully for any sound next door. At exactly three-thirty she heard the faintest noise of a sliding door and a quiet cough. Good. She'd check again tomorrow. The lawn and any other gardening would have to be done before three, or even earlier to be safe. She must get two nice blue pots tomorrow, she thought. She wouldn't bother Frank with those, she could get them in the car and then the next day two palms. If Frank didn't have to be involved he'd never have any idea of the cost. Feeling a bit guilty she turned her mind to tea and what there might be in the freezer that she could defrost in the microwave.

Summer had stretched into autumn and the first rains of the season had softened the soil in the backyard. The best time for planting, Monica knew, and her shrubs spread their roots in their well-prepared beds and the lawn seeds, fertilised and watered every day, pushed their way up to the levelled top soil to the warmth of the sun. The new compost heap in the back corner started with the pile of soil raked off the lawn area and then added to each day with peeling and scraps from the kitchen, began to rot and disintegrate with the weather. Each afternoon at 3.30, after taking Frank's afternoon tea out to the shed, Monica quietly went out to the verandah and sat on the white couch to have her coffee. She listened for sounds from next door but other than the sound of the sliding door and an occasional small cough there was nothing to hear. Monica sat there quietly wondering what the woman next door was doing on her verandah. Was she perhaps having coffee too. What a thought! She wondered what she might be wearing. Probably not a daggy old track suit.

Day by day Monica became more obsessed by the neighbour hidden from her by the high iron fence. She didn't even really know what she looked like or how old she was, having only seen her on a few occasions driving her car. What if she was the same age? What if she was the same height? What did she do out there each afternoon? Once, for a brief moment, Monica thought of making a small hole in the fence with a nail and looking through it to see, but quickly decided against it in case she might get caught. She was amazed at her own curiosity. She had never cared much at all about anyone else's business, but ever since she laid eyes on that verandah next door she'd been consumed by it and then by the person who had created it. Her afternoon television shows were all but forgotten as her obsession became all-consuming and slowly a plan formed that was so bold that it actually made her skin tingle with excitement, the plan to take down the fence and somehow share the life of the woman next door.

Meantime the back verandah of Monica and Frank's house looked a treat. The glass table had been paid off and put in place on the blue and white tiles. Frank and the trailer had been needed for the big round table and chair but there had been no problem about the cost because they'd been on lay-by. By the time Frank knew about them they were already paid for out of housekeeping and he certainly had no complaints about that area – he'd never been fed so well in his life. Whatever was going on with his wife and her absurd need for this back verandah business was beyond his control. He had only sat out there once for morning tea and felt quite silly really. He'd just as soon have morning tea in the shed. He was pleased, though, with what his wife had done with the back yard. It had always been a mess and he'd kept postponing the chore of cleaning it up. He had to admit she'd done a great job with it and he felt a bit mean about leaving her to it, but that was what she was good at. Not him. He was good with wood and quite excited about the rocking horses that he'd finished, ready for painting.

All in all, Frank had accepted the changes in his wife without too much trouble. He certainly didn't understand her anymore but he was enjoying his revitalised sex life and the fabulous meals. As long as she stopped spending money like a lunatic he could handle her new persona and even rather admired her. She'd sure done a good job of that garden for an old girl.

Then came the business about the neighbour's fence and Frank realised he didn't know his new wife at all.

One night over the evening meal Monica suggested and then insisted, in that way of hers, that part of the iron fence between the two houses be pulled down and the brick wall be extended from the front of the house where it finished, the same as every other house in the estate, along and between the two houses as far back as the edge of the back verandah. A completely mad idea, but she insisted on it and he had learned over the past few months that life could be good if she had her way.

He still had bricks left over from the verandah wall, but not enough. It would mean buying more. Another expense. She was at him until he agreed. Then, and this was too much altogether, she wanted him to get permission from the owner. Why couldn't she ask her herself? He didn't even want to build the bloody wall.

Monica was adamant however and in the end he went next door and asked the woman, Mrs Stuck-up if you ask me, about extending the low wall. God, that had been terrible and then to have to go back two days later for her answer. Monica was sure pushing it.

When the old bag next door eventually said yes and Mon was on his back to get started, while waiting for the bricks to arrive he began tearing down the existing iron and wooden railing in preparation.

That was when he saw it, the other verandah.

The same.

Exactly the same.

As far as Frank knew, Monica had never met the neighbour, so when did this little plan get hatched and why didn't she tell him? He looked again next door. The lawn had been in longer, the plants were bigger, especially the trees. But everything else was the same. The couch, the tiles, the table, the one chair. The one chair. He'd asked Mon why there was only one chair and she'd told him the other one was on order, one was all they had. But here in front of him was only one chair. And blue pots and palms. And those cushions.

He swung around and looked at his own verandah. Yes, there were matching cushions. He hadn't even noticed them before.

This was crazy.

Frank stormed inside where Monica was calmly washing the dishes.

"What the hell's going on, Mon?" he demanded. "Why is your new verandah the same as next door's?"

She smiled at him. A sweet smile. A strange smile. A smile that made his skin crawl.

"Because I like next door's," she answered casually. "I wanted one the same."

"But the garden. The garden's the bloody same too,"

"Yes , I like the garden."

And she turned to face him, dish-mop in one hand, dripping water on the floor, smiling that weird smile.

"It's crazy, woman, can't you see that?"

"Does that matter, Frank? Does that really matter to you? You don't have to sit on the verandah if you don't want to."

"Of course I don't want to. Never did really, but certainly not now."

"Well just build the wall then, Frank," she said calmly, turning back to the dishes. "Just build the wall."

"But what about 'er next door," he asked, practically lost for words.

"Obviously she doesn't mind," pointed out Monica. "She said okay, didn't she?"

"Well, she's as mad as you, then," said Frank turning to leave.

"Just build the wall, Frank," she answered flatly and banged a saucepan against the sink so hard that he jumped with the noise.

Unsettled, Frank went down to the pub. As he downed his beer he tried to remember just when he and his wife had become strangers. They'd been living like two flat-mates for years now, neither one really caring about the other. After Peter's death, he thought. That was probably the beginning and since then they'd just sort-of lived together. Even after retirement with Frank in the shed all day or down at the pub and Mon in the house or down the shops they'd become further apart if anything. And now this crazy verandah business. Frank realised he knew nothing about his wife at all.

He returned home by tea-time, a little afraid now of what might happen if he was late. It was the first time that he'd ever been worried about her reaction to anything since they'd been married, and he felt lost and uneasy,

By the end of the week the old fence was down and the foundations laid for the brick one. By the end of the second week the new cream brick low fence was finished. A nice job too.

The subject of the fence had not been raised again. Frank simply built the bloody thing to get a bit of peace, starting the day after their argument. Not even really an argument, he thought, more of an ultimatum, even if un-voiced.

The job gave him the creeps. He never spied anybody from next door during the whole time and even Monica didn't come out to admire and check the progress. As he finished off the back area between the two identical veran-dahs his skin crawled the whole time and he barely raised his eyes from his work afraid to have to acknowledge the existence of this strange new phenomenon.

Monica deliberately stayed inside, other than the nec-essary watering of her new garden which she did early in the morning. She called Frank in for morning tea and lunch with no suggestion of sitting on the verandah for it, much to Frank's relief. He could never ever sit on that verandah now and look across at next door's. The thought gave him the shivers. Nobody had appeared from next door to praise or comment on the fence. He was glad when it was finished and he could return to his shed and his wooden horses.

His relationship with Monica had undergone a not-so-subtle change. Meals were still good, thankfully, but her recent sweetness and new-found sensuality had disappeared. Basically, Frank thought ruefully, things were back to normal. He vowed silently to slip out to the pub a bit more often in the future. A man needed somewhere to relax since his whole world seemed to have gone mad. He felt lost and miserable.

Monica, on the other hand was as excited as a kid waiting for Christmas. She had peered through the kitchen window at 3.30 each day to see if there was any activity on next door's verandah, but with her limited view saw nothing. She knew, or felt, that her neighbour was similarly waiting for the wall to be finished and Frank gone before she came out to sit in the afternoon sun once again.

On the morning after the fence was completed Monica was up at dawn. It was a freezing morning, the beautiful, clear autumn days having caused icy nights. The day was going to be beautiful she could tell by the open sky and by mid-afternoon it should be lovely and sunny on the back verandahs. She swept and wiped the tiles, dusted the tables and fluffed up the cushions. Frank, the thorough workman that he was, had cleaned up his mess behind him and there was little else Monica had to do to set the scene. Next door's verandah, she noted, seemed spotless and she could only guess that her neighbour had cleaned the evening before.

During the morning, skipping the shopping for today, Monica tried on practically everything that was hanging in the wardrobe. What to wear? Something smartish of course but that was difficult since her clothes were plain and inexpensive. After quite some time and allowing for the afternoon warmth, she chose a brown wool skirt and a fawn blouse with a scooped neck. Stockings and her best brown shoes, which needed, and got, a good clean were laid on the bed ready. Would she come out today, Monica wondered. Could it be too soon? What would she be wearing? What did she do out there? Monica forgot Frank's morning tea and could hardly bear to cut him a couple of sandwiches for lunch, she was so excited. She ate nothing herself, afraid she'd vomit, but just had a strong coffee.

The waiting was dreadful. She tried to watch some afternoon soap opera but couldn't concentrate, wondering, wondering.

At 2.30 she showered and dressed and took Frank out a cup of tea and a couple of biscuits. He was heading out to the pub afterwards, he told her, a bit earlier than usual but she was thrilled. It would be a relief not to have him about the place. What if he came out to the verandah after 3.30? He would spoil everything.

"Good idea," she said. "You need a break after all that hard work on the fence. Off you go then," whisking away the half-empty cup, "and have a good time."

Three o'clock. Frank had gone off in the car. All dressed. Make-up, she suddenly thought, panicking. Should she or shouldn't she? Too much or too little? She went into the bathroom and looked at herself in the mirror. Squinting her eyes, she tried to imagine what she'd look like from a distance. Just lipstick today, she decided. Then she'd see.

Three-twenty-five. Monica stood waiting just inside the sliding door, eyes on her watch.

At exactly three-thirty she slid open the door and stepped out on to the verandah. Turning her head to the right she saw a woman step out on to the verandah next door. They glanced briefly at one another and then the woman moved to the couch, placed a glass of wine on the small table next to it and opened the book that she had brought out with her.

Monica froze in horror. Her neighbour was wearing

a beautiful red dress the likes of which she'd never seen. Soft and flowing with a gently frilled neck and draped sleeves. Just beautiful. And she had wine and a book. Monica didn't know what to do. She couldn't just sit down and stare across there. What a fool she was. What had she expected? She didn't drink and Frank only drank beer. She didn't even own a wine glass. Or a book. She didn't read books, only magazines.

Quickly she stepped back inside the door feeling quite sick. She stood there a moment trying to decide what to do. She hadn't done the whole verandah and garden and fence to stand quivering behind the door. But to go back out there ... Suddenly deciding, she quickly filled a glass with water, grabbed a magazine from the lounge, stepped back on to the verandah and sat on the white couch, placing the water on the table beside her.

The woman in the red dress looked up briefly then returned to her book, making no acknowledgment of Monica's presence.

Monica sat there with her head down, pretending to read the magazine, feeling like an idiot. She should have known, she thought grimly, she should have known that she could never belong on such a verandah. She was only Monica and always had been. She would never be any different. But slowly, as time passed, she began to realise that she was different. She had made this verandah, she had made this situation happen. She could follow through on it. And she would. Keeping her head low and looking from the top of her vision she watched the other woman. She noted that her ankles were crossed in a lady-like fashion. Monica crossed her ankles. She watched as the woman stopped reading every now and then and lifted her glass to take a sip of wine, glancing at the garden. Monica sipped her water and looked over at her own garden. It's looking good, she noted, the shrubs had settled in really well and the lawn was beginning to thicken up. She looked at the red dress as carefully as she could without lifting her head, noting every detail. And she sat there, without moving other than to have an occasional sip of water until the woman, after glancing at her watch, replacing the bookmark and closing her book, picking up her now empty glass, rose from the couch and went inside, closing the sliding door behind her. It was exactly five o'clock.

Monica also went inside, shut the door and leant against it, breathing heavily. She must buy a book tomorrow, she thought, and a wine glass and some wine. She didn't know what she could do about clothes though, except that she mustn't wear the same thing again. But that red dress. Oh, if only she had some nice clothes. Well she would get some, she decided, and then realising the time, she quickly changed back into her old clothes, hanging today's carefully on their hangers, and set about preparing tea. As she peeled the vegetables for the casserole and carried the peel down to the compost she smiled gently to herself, pleased. She hadn't got it right today, she knew, but she would get it right. She'd get it perfect. She knew she could.

The following day Monica was down at the mall early checking out the superstores for the red dress but there was nothing like it to be found. She rifled through rack after rack and after several frustrating hours she bought a black skirt in lieu of what she really wanted. She still had to look smart for this afternoon and black seemed to be the safest bet.

It was not an expensive skirt by any means, easily manageable out of housekeeping. She had a black and white checked blouse at home that she'd hardly worn which would look quite classy with the skirt.

Wineglasses, she found, were a nuisance, most of them boxed in sets of six and too many shapes and sizes for her pick from. All that she could remember from the previous afternoon was that the wine was white so she settled for a set that said "white wine" on the box. Then the wine itself. That was a difficult one. Monica had known, since watching her mother wipe herself out every night on alcohol, that she would never drink. But if she was going to do this thing properly she should have a wine. The new rules overran the old and she forced herself to go into the bottle shop and ask for white wine. The bloke in the shop was very helpful, she thought, explaining to him that she didn't drink but wanted something in the house for visitors. Chardonnay, he suggested, was a popular drink for the ladies and could be bought in a cask, a cardboard box, that would last for ages after it had been opened. After getting the instructions on how to open the box, Monica took the cask and glasses out to the car before going back to the bookshop. She didn't really want to be seen carrying alcohol in the mall and was quite relieved to have it safely in the car.

Then the bookshop. Now that was a big surprise. She'd never been inside either of the two bookshops in the mall and was astonished to see how many different books there were. Must be thousands. How on earth could she choose one out of all of these. She approached a counter and asked about gardening books.

"Along that aisle to the left," she was told and going there, she found hundreds of gardening books, all shapes and sizes. Tentatively she picked one out on pruning and looked for a price. Nothing to be seen but a bar code. She took it to the counter and asked the price. Twenty-nine dollars and ninety five cents. Exactly what she had paid for her black skirt. Ridiculous. She inquired if there were cheaper books and was directed to a sales table with a variety of subjects available at much more reasonable prices. Out of her depth completely Monica picked up one with a bright cover of roses and paid for it at the desk. Who on earth read all these books, she wondered. And what book was that woman reading on the verandah? How could she find out?

Realising that she had many things to find out yet Monica drove home with her head in a spin. Books. Who would ever think they'd be such a problem. But she had a tidy new skirt, wine and wine glass and a book to read so she was content enough for the moment.

Feeling good, looking forward to the afternoon, she made Frank a bacon-and-egg sandwich with fried onions, which he loved and had a salad sandwich herself, thinking that she better start keeping an eye on her diet. She could do with being a little thinner, she'd noticed yesterday, looking at the trim figure on the couch next door. It would take some time but she could do it.

With Frank gone down to the pub early again for some reason, she was able to dress at her leisure, eyeing herself in the mirror. Black and white, short sleeves for the afternoon sun and black shoes to match. She brushed her hair thoroughly, picked up her new book and poured herself a glass of wine in one of the new glasses. She sipped it tentatively and pulled a face. Yuk. Why did anybody like this stuff, she thought, let alone drinks heaps of it. But, committed, with glass and book she stepped out on to the verandah at exactly three-thirty.

As Monica shut the door behind her she glanced over at the other verandah and was thrilled to see that her neighbour, closing her own sliding door, was dressed in black and white also. A slightly longer soft black skirt and a finely striped black and white blouse. Long sleeves, unfortunately, but there she was in black and white.

Monica couldn't believe her luck. She moved to the couch, placed her wine glass on the table and sat, with her book on her lap. Ankles crossed. She opened her book and began to read. It was not about roses at all, she found after reading the first few pages, but was a love story. Never mind. She read several pages and then stopped to take a sip of wine.

Glancing across at the other verandah she saw to her pleasure and amazement that the other woman had also picked up her glass and was lifting it in a toasting gesture.

Monica raised her glass and for a second their eyes met,

then the first sip was taken and they both continued reading.

The woman didn't look her way again. Not that Monica saw. But they sipped their wine and read their books until exactly five o'clock and then both women shut their books (Monica had forgotten a bookmark) took their glasses and both re-entered their houses at exactly the same time. Monica plopped on the nearest chair in the dinette, nearly fainting with happiness. She had been acknowledged. She had guessed black and white. She was nearly delirious with joy. Two more days of sun, the forecast had said, and then a change was coming in. What would she wear tomorrow?

She could hardly wait.

WHEN Monica checked the mailbox before going to the mall the next day she found a long envelope with no name and address on it. Puzzled, she opened it to find a beautiful bookmark inside, black with gold writing on it in some foreign language. She swung around to look at the house next door but all she saw from the front was the same two-storey cream-brick house with the lawn and shrubs and garage on the other side as she had always seen. An unremarkable house on an unremarkable street.

Monica stood there a moment, looking up and down the road. Nothing had changed. It all looked the same. But something had changed. She knew and the lady next door knew, their secret hidden away at the back, unseen and unknown by anybody else in the street. Something WONDERFUL had happened and Monica had the proof in her hand, the most beautiful bookmark in the world.

As soon as she was inside Monica took her book out of the linen press to put the bookmark in it. She wasn't quite sure exactly why she'd hidden the book from Frank. What would he care if she bought a book? But somehow it was a secret thing and she wasn't ready yet to share it with anybody. She placed the bookmark at the beginning of chapter two. She had, in fact, already read the first couple of pages of this chapter but hadn't really absorbed them, watching and listening the whole time for movement next door that might indicate the end of the session.

Monica was a slow, laborious reader and it had taken her the whole hour and a half to get through the first chapter. She found, with some surprise, that she was looking forward to the next part of the story. Who'd have thought that she'd ever read a book, let alone like it? She replaced the book carefully so as not to bend the bookmark. She could hardly wait for half past three to come.

At the mall, looking at clothes and frustrated that she hadn't found the red dress, she realised that she couldn't afford any new pieces today. Miffed, and for the first time ever she wished they had more money. She had planned to buy some chicken breasts for a chicken-and-wine dish that she'd seen in a magazine, but, seeing the price of them decided against it. Blow Frank, she thought. He'd seen the cask of wine in the 'fridge and asked her why it was there, knowing that she didn't drink. Her curt answer, "for cooking", had satisfied him, but he'd have to wait a bit longer for his chicken and wine. Bugger it, she thought, she'd just make him a quiche and a steamed pudding. She had all the ingredients at home for that. So she left the mall empty-handed, unfairly furious at Frank because they were short of money.

Once home, though, having vented some of her fury turning over the compost heap, she calmed down a bit and began looking forward to the afternoon, remembering the bookmark. What a lovely gift. What a lovely woman.

Suddenly Monica was hit by a fit of panic. One day she'd find that red dress but would she have the courage to wear it? It would have to be sunny. What might be the reaction from the other verandah? What if the woman was cross about it? What if she stopped coming out in the afternoons? What if? What if? But then, thinking of the book-

81

mark and the raised glass she was sure that it would be all right. Today though, she had better wear something safe and quiet (which was all she had really) and see what happened. She decided on the brown skirt again and, looking up at the clear, warm autumn sun, imagined her long sleeved nylon fawn blouse with it.

Over lunch Frank said that he wouldn't be going to the pub today, he was out of money. Well, thought Monica, you're not the only one and if you think you're getting any from me, you're wrong.

"That's a shame," she said "but it will give you a decent afternoon to finish off the second horse.

"Anyway," she added, "it's only two days to pension day and you can have a little extra then. If you get that horse finished today we might get some paint for them. What do you think?"

"Um," said Frank, disappointed, finishing his coffee. But she was right, he had been a bit slack this week. Still, a couple of beers would've been good. Too much money wasted on useless stuff, he thought, and tramped back to the safety of his shed – the only place that he felt in control nowadays.

With Frank safely at work in the shed Monica prepared herself for the afternoon's adventure. Showered, dressed and groomed, she was waiting at the door at 3.30, book in one hand, glass in the other.

Glancing across at the opposite verandah, she was delighted to see the woman wearing a brown skirt. Her blouse, though, was cream and had a tasteful soft frill falling from the neck. I must get one of those, thought Monica, that's really nice.

They both sat, opened their books and raised the glasses to each other. Monica watched to see what happened to the book mark, and seeing it placed on the couch beside the woman, placed hers similarly and both began reading.

VII

The total picture

MONICA slept late the day after she'd put Frank in the freezer. She stretched luxuriously in the bed and then, suddenly aware that she was naked and without the heavy weight of blankets, she remembered. She lay there quietly for a moment, then stretched again, spreading her arms and legs wide to take up nearly the whole bed. She smiled with pleasure.

For the first time for as long as she could remember she didn't have to get up straight away and make breakfast. And would never have to anymore. She smiled again.

Lying there in luxury, loathe to move, she planned her day.

Today the red dress could be collected. She could hardly wait, but knew that to go too early could mean disappointment. Deliveries were probably made in the morning so she'd go just after lunch. There was no rush, really, she thought, because she couldn't wear it today anyhow. The autumn sun that she'd been enjoying lately on the verandah had given way to soft showers and a drop in temperature. She had hoped the forecast on the tele would be wrong and she could wear the dress immediately, but lying there happily in her bed, too comfortable to move, she could hear the soft patter of rain on the roof. Anyway she needed a lipstick the exact same colour as the dress and would have to look around the mall to find one.

Part of Monica was bitterly disappointed about the weather and not being able to wear the dress immediately,

but another part, the part that stretched so sensuously under the doona, realised that life had changed dramatically, that she was in complete control and there was not any need to rush anything.

She didn't even need to rush Frank, she realised, now that he was safely in the freezer.

Common sense, however, told her that she mustn't leave that job too long. A bit dangerous having a body in the freezer. She'd start that tomorrow, she decided, and put in a couple of hours every day until it was done. Today she better go to the pool shop and buy some acid. And some lime for the compost. And check that new saw of Frank's. See if it would do the job. A soup bone from the butcher should do it, and some frozen mince, she thought cleverly, to test that saw thoroughly.

Then there was the problem of what to wear out to the verandah today. It would be cool. She didn't have too many warm clothes which would be considered tidy or smart, only the one twin-set. Still, with the brown skirt that should be all right. If only she knew where the woman bought her clothes it would be easier. That fancy dress shop, for one, she realised, and decided to look for something more wintry when she went in to get the dress. Yesterday had been pension day and she'd have plenty now to buy some nice clothes. But first the pool shop and the butchers.

Stretching luxuriously once more, surprised at how little muscle soreness she had, considering yesterday's hard work, she rose, showered and dressed in a warm tracksuit and jumper.

Skipping breakfast except for a quick coffee while she made out her shopping list, she backed the car out and headed off to the nursery.

Back home, still well before lunchtime, she took her purchases from the butcher straight out to the shed, anxious to see if she could work the saw and, if she could, if it would do the job. She moved Frank's timber pieces for the horses off the bench, found the switch to the saw and flicked it on. The noise was familiar and not at all frightening, but the thought of putting her hands so close to the rotating teeth was. Still, she'd seen Frank feeding wood through these types of machines for years and if he could do it so could she. Holding the frozen lamb knuckle, which had been her eventual choice for obvious reasons, firmly at each end, she ran it through the saw and cut it neatly in half. To cut it smaller was quite daunting, her fingers too close to the saw for her liking, but gritting her teeth and holding her arms firmly by her side she was easily able to slice a small section from one end of the first cut. This will do fine, she thought, I can do this, and flicking the saw off she took the pieces of knuckle into the kitchen for soup. A big pot of soup, she thought, would last her for meals for ages. She could virtually forget about cooking for days. She peeled all the vegies, put them in the pot and carried the peelings down to the compost. She turned in the peelings and some lime with her big gardening fork. A few fruit trees out the back here eventually, she was thinking, all the compost spread out and dug in carefully. No hurry, though, it would all take time.

Checking her watch, Monica noted that it was nearly twelve o'clock. Time to get tidied to go and collect the red dress. She was soaked from digging at the compost and threw her wet clothes on the laundry floor and dried herself off a bit before looking in the wardrobe to find something tidy to wear into that shop.

Monica opened the wardrobe door in her underwear and stood in front of the sad array of clothes. She caught sight of herself in the mirror that was attached to the inside of one door. She looked at herself for a moment then took off her undies and stood naked before her own image. Too heavy, she thought, but otherwise not bad for her age. She must lose a bit of weight, and probably would without the big carbohydrate meals and meat that Frank loved so much. She ran her hands slowly over her body, feeling the softness of her skin, smooth still except for a bit of wrinkly flesh on the underside of her upper arms. Silk, she thought, I'd like something silk next to my skin. No reason why not, now. More money for herself. She determined to get some silk underwear, pants and petticoat at least. She had no idea if they even made silk bras, but for her heavy breasts she'd need something firm anyway.

Turning to the wardrobe Monica surveyed her choice of clothes. She had never been one to worry much about clothing. As long as she was warm, or cool as the case may be, she had been satisfied. Style, per se, meant little to her and the changing fashions that she saw on the young ones had little to do with her. Once or twice in the magazines she had seen a dress or coat that took her fancy, but having nowhere to wear them they seemed a waste and she'd never even bothered to try one on. Looking now at her miserable rack of boring and cheap attire she knew that this would have to change. She had the verandah now.

Thinking of the verandah, she chose the best she had under the circumstances; her black skirt and the tan twin-set, stockings and her best black shoes with a small heel. Dressing quickly, concerned about the time, she checked herself out again in the mirror. Yes she was tidy enough for the shop, but not fashionable. Still that would change.

At the mall Monica went straight to the fancy little boutique. As soon as she entered it her good mood of the day disappeared instantly and she had to control herself to stop running out into the safety of the shopping crowds. Looking far calmer than she felt she approached the stony-faced assistant at the little counter.

"I've come for my red dress," she said "I ordered it a couple of days ago."

"Oh yes, madam, the red crepe. It arrived this morning. Would you like to try it on?"

"No thank you," replied Monica, anxious to leave the shop. "I'll be fine." And as the assistant brought it from the back and wrapped it in tissue she looked at it apprehensively, hoping that it would actually fit her. She had been to the bank machine and had the cash out ready before the dress was wrapped. Hastily she left the shop, the precious parcel in a fancy bag with the name of the boutique printed tastefully across it.

Back in the throng of shoppers, breathing easily again, Monica felt a tremendous surge of pride. The saleswoman had treated her quite courteously and Monica had handed over the outstanding $420 as if she did it every day. Four hundred and twenty dollars. The contents of her entire wardrobe wouldn't be worth much more than that.

She clutched the handles of the bag more tightly and headed towards one of the specialist make-up counters in one of the larger stores. Usually she picked up a lipstick or two when a basket of oddments was put out on special at the chemist. She had never cared too much about colours as long as they weren't bright red which she had felt wouldn't suit her, Now, however, she was not only going to buy a bright red lipstick but she was going to buy an expensive one.

At the counter she carefully unwrapped and displayed her new red dress to the young girl working there. A matching colour was soon found and with her two precious purchases in hand Monica took herself to the fancy coffee shop for a flat white and a toasted sandwich. She was quite hungry really, having not eaten yet that day and spoiled herself with a Danish pastry. Yummy, she thought, her diet could start another day. Today was special.

Taking great care not to get the dress wet, waiting patiently outside the mall under the verandah until there was a break in the showers, Monica made a dash for the car and returned home with plenty of time to spare before three-thirty. Many other folk had been standing there waiting for the rain to stop. Monica wondered if any of them should have looked her way how could they possibly have guessed what she was carrying in that bag and where she was going to wear it. It had been a strange thought for her to have and she became excited even acknowledging the existence of such a thought. She had glanced furtively to each side but nobody had been taking any notice of her at all. They had no idea, she thought, that she lived such an exciting life.

Back home, the dress hanging from the door frame between the dinette and lounge, where she could see it all the time, she poured her glass of wine, picked up her book from the dinette table and waited for her watch to show three-thirty. She was looking forward to continuing her book. The story was beginning to get really interesting and she wanted to see what happened next. She had picked it up a couple of times, tempted to read on, but didn't want to spoil the specialness of the verandah and had reluctantly put it down again.

At three-thirty on the dot, Monica stepped on to the verandah, put her wine on the small table, only just out of reach of the softly falling rain and sat on the white couch. She put her book on her lap, opened it and put the bookmark on the seat next to her, raised her head to see the woman on the opposite verandah, raised her glass in a shared toast, replaced the glass and began reading.

She didn't care that her choice of skirt had been wrong. The tan twin-set was spot on and she was pleased enough with that. She had to admit, though, that her neighbour's matching tan skirt made her whole outfit look like a suit. And a coloured scarf around the neck with shades of tan, gold, black and white. Monica thought she must look at a few scarfs; they would certainly brighten up some of her drab clothes.

For today, though, Monica was content enough. With the red dress hanging in the dinette ready for tomorrow's sun.

Tomorrow.

On the following afternoon the sun was out again and the skies were back to blue. It would be warm and very pleasant on the verandah.

This was the day.

This was the day to wear the red dress.

Monica had decided quite early in the morning, even before she started on Frank in the shed. The early morning sky had been cloudless and although the crispness in the air had sent her back to the house for a cardigan, she knew that by three-thirty the autumn warmth would definitely warrant the wearing of her new purchase.

All day she'd been on tenterhooks, anxious for the time to come, wondering what the women next door could possibly wear on such a beautiful day. It had been one week exactly since she'd worn the red dress and it was possible on such a day that she might wear it again.

When Monica stepped out on to the verandah she couldn't stop herself from glancing quickly to her left, before moving to the couch. She nearly dropped her glass of wine on the blue and white tiles. There she was and SHE WAS WEARING THE RED DRESS. Nearly fainting, Monica continued to the couch, sitting and putting the wine on the table all in one movement. Her legs were so weak they hardly seemed to hold her up and her heart was beating so wildly she thought it would burst.

With her head held low while she gained her composure, she opened her book, placed the bookmark aside, took hold of her glass and looked up.

There it was, the mirror image verandah just as she had dared to imagine it. The woman on the opposite verandah, dressed in the same red dress, book on her lap, lifted her glass to Monica with a wry smile. The two women's eyes met for a moment then the woman sipped her wine, replaced her glass on her table and began reading. Monica could not concentrate on her book even though she had been looking forward to continuing the story. She sat there as if in shock, her ankles crossed and the book open below her dropped head. What now? She felt frozen in time, unable to move. When should she pick up her glass? Could she even pick it up without dropping it? What would tomorrow be like, with no red dress? Thinking of the dress she moved her gaze from the book to her knees and the beautiful, soft fabric that covered them. The brightness of the red reassured her. It had only taken her one week to match clothes. She could do it again. She would do it again. There was no real rush. Gradually she would buy the clothing she saw on the other verandah. Already she had begun looking for that cream blouse with the soft frill. It would all be exactly right eventually.

Relaxed now, Monica took a sip of the wine and, joy of joys, the woman opposite was doing the same. Who was reading whose mind, she wondered for a second, then, back to her usual placid manner, put it down to coincidence and began reading.

The hour and a half went quickly, Monica once again absorbed in her story. She was alerted to the time by a short cough from the opposite verandah. Guiltily, she replaced her bookmark, took her glass, still half-full, and moved to the door just in time. Half-turning her head to the right she watched the other red dress move inside and attuned her actions to match. Oh, the joy of it. Inside, the door shut behind her, she leant against the frame and emptied the contents of the glass in one gulp.

With her eyes closed she stood there for some time lost in the memory of the last hour and a half.

She was so excited that she didn't know what to do with herself. Excitement was a completely new emotion to her, only experienced since she first looked over the fence and saw the verandah. Today, though, was a different sort of excitement and she was loathe to let go of it and return to the hum-drum routine of tea and telly.

She poured herself another glass of wine and sat at the table in the dinette sipping it quite quickly, looking out on to her wondrous verandah and the white couch where she had been sitting only moments ago in the red dress.

She had never had two glasses of wine before. She still didn't like the taste, much too sour, but she liked the warm feeling that it gave her and today, today she wanted to keep that feeling for a bit longer.

When the wine was finished, Monica went into the bedroom, opened the wardrobe door and looked at herself in the mirror. She lifted her arms and ran her hands down the full length of her torso, over her breasts and stomach to her thighs. The fabric felt so soft and beautiful, but to her horror she noticed two dark sweat marks under her arms. It had not been warm enough to cause sweating but her emotions must have got the better of her. Would the stains have been noticeable from next door? The thought was horrific. She positioned her arms as they would have been for reading and was relieved to see nothing of the stain. Well this dress will have to go straight to the dry cleaners, she thought, far too scared to handle the fabric herself. Usually, with her good clothes on for only an hour and a half they could be simply hung to air, but not today's. Dry cleaner tomorrow.

Taking the dress off, loathe for it to leave her body, Monica realised that she was a bit tipsy. She felt good though and thought a small lie-down would be pleasant. She stripped off and naked, warm and comfy under the light doona, she stretched and ran her hands once again over her body. Softly, softly over and around her breasts. Her skin felt good and so did she. Moving her hands to her stomach and thighs she realised to her surprise that she was feeling a bit sexy. How nice to stroke her own body. Soft hands on soft flesh, gentle and pleasurable. So different to Frank's harsh hands and heavy touch. She began to explore the area between her thighs which, to date, she'd only touched for a cursory wash. Caught up in the moment and the wine, the excitement of the afternoon having pushed her to an unfamiliar place of pleasure, Monica masturbated to orgasm and fell blissfully asleep, her old face softened and sweet like that of a young girl.

Orgasm was a new experience for Monica. After more than forty years of sex with Frank, a duty to be performed, no more no less, she had at last found the secret pleasure of womanhood. Over the years she had read articles in the magazines about orgasm, but no-one seemed to be able to really describe it and she had no idea whether the occasional bit of pleasure she sometimes felt with Frank was 'it'. Mostly with Frank she had felt nothing, as in the other areas of her life. Especially since Peter's death. Life was just something you went through, one day after the other, plodding along until you died. Sex had always been the same. Plodding along until Frank finished.

It had been quite a day for Monica.

VIII

The gift

WHEN Miss Trante went inside at five o'clock she was tempted for the first time to glance across at Monica doing the exact same thing. She sensed, rather than saw, the flash of bright red going inside next door. She found herself both furious and elated at the same time. With her strong intelligence she realised this perplexing mix of emotions was for her a gift. She felt very much alive for a seventy-year-old, more alive than she'd felt for some time.

How the devil, she wondered, did that woman find the same dress? How the devil could she afford it? She was too plump to carry it off well but one certainly had to give her 'A' for effort. Well, well, what a turn-up. Daddy would have loved it.

Pouring herself another glass of wine, Miss Trante sat at her dining-room table and looked out through the French doors to her verandah. Little had she thought when she decorated that verandah that this scenario could ever take place. Or that she herself would be a party to it. This last week had been extraordinary and she'd found herself looking forward to her afternoon sojourns on the verandah with great anticipation. Every day a new adventure. She wondered, if right at that very moment, the woman next door was sitting at a table having a second glass of wine looking out on her own verandah. She tried to imagine the inside of her neighbour's house, but doubted that it could possible be anything like her own. For one thing

nobody else would have the same furniture, most of it her imported treasures. Anyway, by the look of the woman in her other clothes and the look of that old builder husband of hers she would imagine that there wouldn't be much money around over there.

One thing she did know though was that she had to stay in charge. She could not be outdone by this woman, though she seriously doubted the chance of that happening. Nevertheless, bit by bit, she must run the game. In fact, she congratulated herself, she'd already started by putting that bookmark in the letter box. That was brilliant. Perhaps a book suggestion next. God knows what on earth her neighbour was reading. By the look of her you'd imagine she'd only read the odd magazine.

Going to the bureau, she fossicked around awhile and found the newest catalogue from the bookshop. She had nearly finished the book she was reading and was due for a new one on her next trip to the city.

Miss Trante only shopped in the city and only once a week. She hated the local mall with a vengeance; full of noisy, smelly teenagers and local women gossiping in groups and pulling small children along by the arm. And the noise, not to mention the sickly smell of doughnuts and popcorn. She had been there once, to see, hoping for something better but had come away disgusted, vowing never to go back again. The city, though, was different. One could choose which shops one liked, the quiet shops with room to move and genteel assistants. All of her shopping, including her weekly food supplies, was done in the city. Her hairdresser of some twenty years was in the city. Her doctor, although only seen every couple of years for a check-up, was in the city. Her health was extremely good, especially for her age and the only thing that she'd really needed him for had been vaccination shots for overseas trips. Yes, she would go to the bookshop on her next visit to town and buy that new biography. Perhaps a novel as well, as one book hardly lasted her a week. As well as her afternoon reading time on the verandah, after a lie-down following lunch, she liked to read a chapter or two before sleep.

So tomorrow she'd put the catalogue in next door's letter box with the biography circled. Tonight in fact, after dark, ready for tomorrow's mail collection. She was due to go to town the day after that and that would allow Mrs Blob next door only a day to find the book. We'll see exactly what she's made of, she thought maliciously, but at the same instant, conversely, she rather hoped that the woman would have the book in her hand when she stepped onto the verandah in two day's time.

The thought opened up a whole new aspect to the verandahs and the afternoon ritual. Clothes catalogues for a start, wine lists, crystal glass outlets, shoe shops. Oh, she could build this woman brick by brick. Hairdressers, make-up, education through reading. She was unable to visualise where all of this would lead, but for the moment the idea of being in charge again and the bizarre circumstances that had brought the situation about were enough to give her a feeling of well-being, purpose and authority.

Carefully Miss Trante circled the cover and description of the book in red on the catalogue, then placed it in a plain envelope on the table, ready to be slipped into next door's letter box before she went to bed.

Well satisfied with her day, she made herself a light meal which she ate at the table, leafing through an *Australian Vogue* as she ate, checking what clothes might be suitable for the cooler months to come. There is no hurry, she reasoned, shutting the glossy magazine and pushing it aside. There is plenty of time ahead to play this little game and to rush it would be foolish. She would take her time and slowly, slowly manage the scene (which she had inadvertently started with her little verandah) to her own satisfaction.

Although her health was exceptional for her age, or so she considered, Miss Trante was noticing a few changes here and there that she definitely was not pleased with. She was finding that she really needed that little afternoon nap after lunch and was quite annoyed about it. Her legs were getting tired too often for her liking and so were her eyes. To date she hadn't needed glasses, but if she read for too long she found that she'd get a headache and at night particularly when she read every evening before sleep her eyes would lose focus and she'd have to stop. Of course, a decent reading light in the bedroom would help. She'd have to look into that one day in the city. But then, she had to admit, she was ready to sleep much earlier nowadays so perhaps it didn't matter. Reading on the verandah was no problem, the natural light facilitating easy vision and she treasured her afternoons on the couch. Only recently she had considered even cutting that hour and a half down to an hour because she was finding that her neck was beginning to bother her. But since that woman next door had opened up this new adventure she'd put it off.

Miss Trante pondered on limiting the verandah time to an hour. Fairly soon. That would give her another chance to take charge of the situation. She was pretty damned sure that that woman wouldn't dare to stay outside for an extra half hour on her own. She would guess that she was quite a bit younger than herself and probably didn't have any trouble with her damned neck. Probably didn't need a lie-down after lunch either. Bloody woman.

Miss Trante was not liking growing old, even though she was faring quite a bit better than others she'd seen in the city with their canes and their walkers. In a way, though, she thought, a nice cane could look rather smart and she had a few beauties from her travels. But the tiredness was a nuisance. Getting meals was sometimes such a bother that now and then she skipped tea altogether. Lunch was now her main meal and she was still fresh enough at that time of the day to fiddle around in the kitchen.

The food business annoyed her immensely. She was extremely fussy about her food, with a penchant for Asian and Japanese dishes which she had learnt to make most successfully for herself. With old age creeping upon her she often wondered just how she would cope later on. Frozen meals were out of the question and so, most definitely, were Meals on Wheels.

Sometimes lately, Miss Trante thought about folk with big families and the back-up that might be available when growing old. Children and grandchildren visiting and helpful. Siblings to share problems with on the 'phone. People around. How wonderful that would be. But then, she treasured her solitude, answerable to nobody and having complete control over her time. She would be loathe to give that up and have to accommodate the needs of others. What a dreadful thought.

Miss Trante's mother had died when only two years older than she was now. But she had not been a strong woman and had indulged her body to the point of stupidity. Their last few years of living together before the old girl had a stroke and then two months later, a fatal heart attack, had been abysmal. Mother had smoked incessantly, drunk far too much far too often and ate atrocious food full of fat and carbohydrate. Unhappy at still being alone after a string of failed affairs, the once happy-go-lucky beauty had become bitter and more self-indulgent than ever. During the years that the mother and daughter shared their rented townhouse, there were often heated disagreements about each other's habits and fetishes. They did not love each other in the normal sense, rather putting up with each other because they were family and otherwise alone.

School holidays and a treasured trip away on a regular basis kept Miss Trante sane, the break away from her demanding parent a breath of fresh air amid the stale relationship between the two women.

Miss Trante buried her mother with proper decorum but never grieved for her. Seven years later when her father passed away from cancer in his early eighties she wept inconsolably and had to take four weeks' leave from school to fly to Paris for the funeral and try and pull herself together enough to continue work, feeling more alone in the world than she thought possible.

She had spent her final holiday with him in France where he had retired to a tiny *pension* near the ocean and although he was quite ill at the time they had taken walks together along the beach and laughed at memories of their many shared journeys, enjoying each other's company as they always had.

Trips away were never the same without Daddy to share them but they were her life's habit and every cent she earned went into travel until she retired from her position and found the manageable two-storey house in the estate.

Bother tired legs and a stiff neck, she thought, she could deal with those and must have many good years ahead before she seriously had to worry about the future. The immediate future, the moulding of her neighbour and their shared experience bordering slightly on insanity, was looking good. Like a marvellous book, Miss Trante could not wait for the next chapter.

MONICA had allowed herself two hours' work in the shed each morning until she was finished. Her life was falling into a new pattern that she found manageable and pleasant. A lazy lie-in 'till about half past eight or nine. A quick trip to the mall for shopping and then a pleasant morning tea in the coffee shop instead of a breakfast at home.

Check the mail on the way inside, deal with the bills, then an hour or two in the garden, keeping the front tidy and gradually preparing the back and the compost heap for fruit trees next autumn. A lazy lunch with a bit of tele and then work in the shed, stopping always in time to shower and dress before three-thirty. After the verandah at five, a change of clothes to old comfy favourites and until she felt like bed and a chapter of her newest book.

The work in the shed had not proved quite as easy-going as she thought after playing with the soup knuckle. Small things like fingers were quite difficult, afraid the whole time that she'd lose her own. Larger areas, like thighs, were hard to cut in small slices. Slowly and carefully though, she managed to work out compromises here and there and on the whole was making good progress. Frank had kept all his wooden off-cuts in four large plastic buckets with handles and lids. Monica could lift these fairly easily while they were filled with wood, so she allowed a half-full limit for her acid which would have to be carried to deep holes that she planned to dig about the yard. The grisly bags of gut had been the first to leave the freezer and would be the quickest to dissolve she figured, which left only two buckets for the rest. Not nearly enough. She decided to stop and give herself a break when these two were filled as they would need to be left for quite some time for the acid to do its work. If she couldn't get finished by the end of winter, she thought, she'd have to leave the rest until the following winter, the warmer weather being bad for odours.

It was cold in the shed as winter drew closer and she had to wear one of Frank's old jumpers to keep warm. The gruesome nature of her work didn't worry her at all. It was simply a job that had to be done. Standing at the saw, day after day, Monica thought of nothing but clothes. What she might wear that afternoon and how close it would be to that on the other verandah. And then there were the books as well, books full of real people's lives and thoughts, books that made her head reel with possibility and sometimes a sadness for her own wasted life.

Monica had become an avid reader. Ever since the first biography, she began reading at night as well as on the verandah. Her television was off more than on nowadays. Snuggled early into bed with her book had become a habit that she loved and each time she went to the bookshop to buy the indicated choice on the catalogue that appeared weekly in her letter box, she chose another book at random for herself. She loved to read and couldn't understand how she had spent practically a lifetime without books.

Monica now went into the city once a fortnight. The clothes, marked in red, photographed on glamorous young models on the pages of *Australian Vogue* that also appeared regularly in her letter box, were only to be found in the large prestigious city stores. Monica would spend a whole morning wandering through the ladies' departments, admiring the fashions and feeling the fabrics. She'd already found, and bought, a cream blouse with a soft frill falling from the neck, a tan skirt to match the twin-set and a beautiful soft scarf in tan, gold, black and white. She always went on pension day, with money to spend, albeit carefully, and had a nice lunch in a small Italian restaurant before returning home.

Monica's best clothes, and the best of her old, hung on a clothes rack in the dinette. Some hung from the lounge room door and some were folded neatly on the dinette table which she kept meticulously clean. According to the weather and her instinct, which was becoming uncannily correct, she would be dressed and ready for the verandah at three-thirty. If, when she stepped out on to the blue and white tiles, she glimpsed a different outfit from that which she wore, she shot back in and changed more quickly than any woman could imagine. Then she'd return, sit on the couch and raise her glass to her neighbour, who would be waiting for her, glass at the ready.

The women had changed their positions on the lounges to the cushions nearest the house since the colder weather had arrived. This kept them out of the wind and rain, still comfortable and continuing their ritual without being affected by the weather. The smaller glass tables had been pulled around against the front of the white couch nearest the edge of the verandah where their wine would be safe from the elements. There was just room, looking past the larger glass tables and chairs to see each other clearly but they couldn't wait for the more clement weather of spring to return to their usual seats.

Monica thought at one stage, on a particular nasty winter day, when the wind pulled at the pages of her book, that it would be nice to fill-in the back edge of the verandah with tall sliding glass doors that could be closed in winter to keep the elements out and opened on the warmer days. Until the woman across the brick wall decided to do just that, Monica had to put it out of her mind. There was not a chance in the world of her instigating even the smallest change unless it first happened across the way.

The suburb around them was quiet at this time of the year. Instead of the evening barbecues, wafting the odours of fat and onions along the rows of houses, the families were tucked inside early as dark fell earlier and earlier. Cars still came and went, swishing water from the overflowing gutters, but the noisy children had all disappeared inside by their fires and computers for the majority of the winter months.

Only on two back verandahs, unknown and unseen, did everything stay basically the same, no matter what the weather. Warm woolly jumpers and smartly tailored wool slacks kept the two women cosy in their own sheltered corners and white wine turned to red for the winter months.

Monica's cask of white had long since been poured over casseroles as lists of wine with particular bottles circled in red had appeared in her letter box. She was just acquiring a taste for the pleasant rieslings and semillons when to her surprise her neighbour appeared on the verandah with a glass of red wine. Monica had noticed the shiraz circled on the last list but had thought it was a mistake, all the previous bottles having been white.

So next day she bought the shiraz and was pleasantly surprised at her first sip to taste and feel the warmth of the new drink. She tried several different red wines over the winter months, some of which she liked and some of which she didn't, but if a new one was indicated on the wine ads that were slipped into her letter box every now and then she always felt obliged to buy it, try it.

One morning, early in winter, when Monica went out the front to check the letter box she was delighted to find a beautiful blue and white pot on her small front porch. It was identical to the pot on the round table next door. Over the past weeks Monica had become aware that the pot on her table, although blue and white and similar in shape, was not exactly the same as that on the opposite verandah. She had not known what to do about it; the one she had was the closest copy that she'd been able to find. Holding the gift in her hand, Monica was deeply touched. The pot was half the weight of her own and the blue images on the fine white china were delicate and beautiful. She went to the verandah and swapped the pots. Immediately she was aware of the poor quality of the original pot that she held in her hand. Ashamed, she threw it in the rubbish. Well, she hadn't known much back then, she thought. What a thick-head she must have seemed. And how wonderful was her neighbour to giver her such an expensive gift. She had no idea what to do in return, or even if she should do anything at all. She was not used to receiving gifts; Frank usually gave her a card for birthdays and Christmas. Peter sometimes had given her gifts on special occasions, once even, on Mother's Day, a big bunch of flowers wrapped in beautiful cellophane had been delivered to her door by a florist. But that was a long time ago.

Thinking of Peter and feeling a bit melancholy and emotional, Monica went into the spare room just to see if one of the cards he had made when he was in junior school might have been saved and packed away.

Absently she picked up Pete's biology book from the floor where she had hastily thrown it after her work with Frank in the bath was finished. She opened the box it came from to replace it, but saw a smaller book among the pile and picked it up. It was a half-empty photo album. She had forgotten about it. Opening it, she found eight or nine photos of the last fishing trip Pete made with his mates. They were silly photos; boys with underpants on their heads, somebody passed out drunk, another boy proudly holding a fish about six centimetres long and then one of Pete, his cap on sideways and pulling a stupid face.

Monica started to cry. She sat on the nearest box with the silly photos held in her lap and cried like she'd never cried before. In fact, she never had before. Ever. Perhaps when she was little, until she learned how much it angered her mother, but never since. Not even when they showed her the photos of the car, wrapped around the tree, practically unrecognisable. She hadn't cried when she and Frank stood by the window at the morgue and identified his mangled body. But she cried now. She sobbed and she screamed. She collapsed off the box into a heap on the floor, weak as a kitten, sobbing, sobbing into the old carpet square on the floor. Peter, Pete. Her baby. She hadn't even cried when he was born. Or groaned. Or screamed. Just grunted once and pushed. Oh, Peter.

She lay there sobbing until she was too exhausted to cry anymore, and slept where she lay, depleted. A tired, sad old piece of humanity, free at last of some of the pain that had festered inside her for so many years.

IX

The crystal goblets

MONICA'S wardrobe grew immensely during the winter months with trips to the city an absolute pleasure on rainy days. She could park in the large undercover parking stations and go straight to the shops in the lift, out of the weather and into the air conditioned stores. And she loved the winter clothes; soft mohair jumpers, smart, warm tailored skirts and slacks and even an alpaca vest, circled on a *Vogue* page from the letter box.

A warm, coffee-scented brasserie in the four-storey shopping centre where she parked had become a favourite for good coffee and a choice of the variety of hot treats that they served for lunch before going home to her afternoon chore in the shed.

There were big bookshops in the city too, bigger than ever she could have imagined. Thousands and thousands of books on every subject under the sun. Monica often wandered around the aisles, touching a book here and there, even picking one up occasionally and sniffing the wonderful smell of new ink on paper. She would watch other people choose a book and when they moved away she'd go and see which one they'd taken, pick it up and read the book cover. Sometimes, if she read a page or two and became interested, she would buy the book to read in bed. She could spend hours in the bookshops fascinated by the different sections and variety of covers. Who wrote all these books she would wonder and why did they write

them? Who read them all? How long did they last and how many people read the same book before it fell to pieces? She remembered the school library and how much she hated the lessons that were spent there and how boring she thought the whole place was. Nowadays, she thought, she'd love to go back there when it was empty and have a good look around.

Monica had recently bought a smallish bookcase herself which she'd put in the lounge room. Her tiny collection of books didn't even fill one shelf but she was very proud of it and looked forward to filling every shelf with books that she'd read.

She had been going to throw out the first one that she'd bought on special. The love story. She could tell already, just in the short time that she'd been introduced to quality books by Mrs Next Door, that it wasn't a very good book. She didn't quite know how she knew. In the beginning she had enjoyed that story, but now she knew that it was a simple story and not well written. There was something about the way the words were put together that was very ordinary. Monica felt very guilty daring to think that she might criticise that book, or any other book. Heavens, less than a year ago she hadn't ever read a book other than at school. What a cheek she had. But even though part of her dared to rate the romance novel as not good enough she found that she was unable to throw it out. After all, it was a book and she had read it, so it went on to the bookshelf along with the others.

Monica had written quite a long letter to Frank's brother in England. As well as telling him a little about the latest book she was reading at the time, she had written at length about a fictitious weekend holiday that she and Frank had taken in Queensland. At the same time, smiling to herself, she had recognised that it was a bit like writing a book, she supposed, except much shorter. She was getting a bit above herself, she thought suddenly, to even imagine for a moment that she might compare herself in even the smallest way to those who were clever enough to write books. What a pity, though, that she had no one else to write to. She'd quite enjoyed making up the holiday.

Monica had no idea where her brother and sister lived. If they were even alive. She had only seen them once since her wedding day and that had been at the invitation of her sister Liz (quite a flash one it was, too, with gold lettering and fancy edges) to her own wedding. The ceremony was held in a large church and Monica was surprised to see how many people were there. She knew nothing about her siblings and had never bothered to get to know them or anything about them since leaving home. It was obvious to Frank and Monica that Elizabeth was marrying well and was, in her own right, admired and respected by many of those at the wedding.

At the reception afterwards, a sit-down dinner in a very fancy restaurant, Monica and Frank, sitting at a table with brother Bill, his girlfriend and four people that they'd never met before, both wished they could run away. They felt awkward and out of place with no understanding of the speeches and the people and the places that were referred to. At the earliest possible time they left, making promises to Bill to keep in touch and give their love to Liz who was impossible to speak to, seated with the toffs at a long table out in front of everybody. They were glad to get out of there and home to their lounge room and tele, Frank flopping into his chair with a can of beer and Monica into hers with a cup of tea. They knew their place.

Since the wedding Mon had never heard from Bill or Liz and even though she had Bill's address, at that time, she hadn't contacted them either. Now though, she thought, she wouldn't mind writing them a letter. A made-up letter full of stories of success and excitement. If she knew where to send it. And what, then, if they decided to visit? What a thought. Of course she could put a made-up address at the top, somewhere romantic and interesting, far away from their little house at the estate. Fiction, fiction, fiction.

That's the area of the bookshop where that letter would go, Monica laughed out loud at the thought, pleased with herself. Perhaps she'd do it one day, just for fun..

Fun had never played much of a part in Monica's life and the concept was new to her. To do something just for fun. How changed her life had become.

Just imagine, she chuckled to herself, that at this time last winter she hardly moved from the gas-heater in the lounge room and the television. She imagined that she should have been bored out of her wits, but since her whole life had been boring, looking back now, she supposed that she hadn't even noticed.

This winter, whatever the weather, she looked forward every day to that hour and a half on the back verandah. Looked forward to reading. Looked forward to a glass of red wine. Looked forward to clothing herself in warm, comfy garments and sitting outside snuggled in the corner of the couch just out of reach of the weather. Except, she had to admit, some days the wind whipped right into her cosy corner making it not only difficult to turn pages but cutting like ice into her face and hands so that she was nearly frozen by the time she went inside.

Stubbornly, neither woman would give in to the weather, no matter how cold it was. The game was being truly tested, each one waiting to see if a particularly cold or stormy day might stop the other coming out. But Miss Trante's absolute determination to keep control at all costs and Monica's blind devotion to the thrill of the afternoon affair, ensured that the two old women practically ignored the weather, each determined to sit on their respective couches no matter what.

Miss Trante, with an eye to the elements, had chosen their clothing very wisely and their bodies were amply protected from the cold. A spencer underneath the thick jumpers and vests wasn't out of the question either. Warm hats, and gloves, a must for those who braved the cold Victorian winter, were out of the question. Far too undignified. Before Monica's verandah had materialised she had often chosen to stay indoors on a particularly nasty day and read at the dining room table, she stubbornly refused to be the first to break the tradition.

Both woman, in fact, found themselves enjoying the majority of the winter days, exposed to thunder and lightning and whatever else nature threw their way. There was an element of danger and excitement sitting out there in a storm and both of them, too elderly one would think to enjoy a rush of adrenalin, thrived on the experience.

But eventually winter ran its course and the sweet smells of pollen heralded the beginning of spring.

With the change in the weather came a change in clothes. Back to skirts and blouses; bright coloured florals and stripes now rather than the plain unchallenging colours of the year before.

Various good quality wines appeared in the crystal goblets that were now used on both verandahs.

This was yet another new aspect to the game. As well as guessing what Mrs Next Door might be wearing (and Mon was getting uncannily good at this) the choice of red or white wine had to be made and the appropriate goblet used. It didn't take Monica long to find a way of handling this particular problem. Next to the sliding glass door, on the breakfast bar, she'd prepare a white wine in its proper goblet and a red in the same. She had learnt (via the letter box) the difference between a red goblet and a white one and was prepared after the day she took a red out on a warm spring afternoon and saw with horror a goblet of white on the opposite verandah. Well, she was soon ready for that little trick. How good she was getting at this.

Both women had been to the hairdressers for a shorter cut, baring their necks to the welcome warmth of the spring sunshine. Monica had always worn her hair shoulder length and straight. She had been aware that her neighbour's hair was much shorter than her own but hadn't really considered changing her hairstyle until a hairdresser's card appeared in the letter box.

The winter's growth on the shrubs in both gardens was quite noticeable and buds were popping out here and there ready to burst open in their brilliant colours to frame each verandah with a stunning display.

Monica's compost heap had grown immensely. Every couple of weeks she would buy more soil from the nursery and add it to the pile, turning it over with her fork. Her plan was to eventually spread it over the rear section of the backyard and dig it in thoroughly. Three fruit trees, peach, nectarine and apricot would be planted there with some low ground covers to fill in between. Monica liked stone fruit and was an expert at preserving. She was hoping that at some time in the future she'd be able to share her preserves with next door, as a thank-you for the gifts and advice she'd received. Could she dare to be so bold? Preserves were only preserves after all. But that fruit was a long way off yet and that decision could be shelved for the moment.

To her surprise, doing Frank had taken much less time than she'd expected and she was long finished before the seasons changed. She'd become extremely adapt at using the band saw and found that she could whizz through a limb in no time, any flat slabs being cut and recut so that only small pieces went into the acid buckets. She'd had to buy two more buckets to be sure of complete saturation and was content enough with the result, in fact amazed at how quickly the small portions disintegrated.

Frank's head had been the worst. Not only because it was Frank's head (because severed and frozen it looked nothing like Frank) but because it was such a width across and roundish, difficult to hold steady. After some contemplation she cut it once longways which made the whole job much simpler and she'd been pleased with herself for thinking of that.

Monica was, in fact, a very practical person. Working out basic problems came easily to her and this ability proved a godsend with her work in the shed.

She had learned about hydrochloric acid years ago when she was working at the nursery. There were not as many shops around that catered solely to swimming pools back in those days and the nursery carried a small stock of skimmers, vacuums, chlorine, salt and acid. She had been told over and over again how dangerous that acid was and never to touch it. "Dissolve anything," Mr Jason had said. "Never get it on your hands, for goodness sake or they'll disappear before your eyes!" Buying the acid from pool shops and hardware stores had not been any sort of problem, although she varied her suppliers just in case.

The contents of the buckets, once the tiny fragments were dissolved, had been poured into half a dozen fairly deep holes spread around the backyard and then filled in with dirt. When the weather was good Monica planned to spread her compost over the yard and plant low native ground covers to fill in the spaces between the fruit trees. She would do that soon, she decided, as a sort-of end to the whole job. And get those fruit trees in. The shed had been cleaned and tidied, the plastic buckets left upside down on the soil to drain and stacked neatly away inside a cupboard. She only went out there now for gardening tools, the shed being now simply a shed bereft of any reminiscence of Frank at all. Frank was quite simply not a part of her life anymore other than infrequent letters to his brother to answer any that came in the post.

Monica's life now consisted of afternoons on the verandah and various ways of filling in the time before and after that precious hour and a half. Shopping and reading took up the majority of her day, with some time spent gardening according to the weather. She now took meticulous care of her clothing, her new clothes especially, keeping them freshly washed and ironed on hanging racks in the dinette and stacked neatly in careful piles on the table, ready for a quick change if necessary. Every time a brochure appeared in the now regular unmarked envelope in her letter box, she would make a trip to the city to search out the blouse, jumper, skirt, dress or accessories that were ringed in red. She liked the accessories best now and spent hours rifling through scarf after scarf, sometimes even buying one that hadn't been suggested by next door, feeling guiltily pleased at her own audacity..

Books, though, had become her main love, a fascinating obsession above and beyond that of clothes and fabrics. She practically haunted the large bookshops in the city, wandering slowly around them for hours at a time, breathing in the smells, absorbing the colours shapes and sizes. Looking, touching and holding any book that especially caught her eye, weighing its contents, guessing at the knowledge it held.

One cold day, towards the end of winter, filling in the morning in the city, Monica decided to go to the State Library. A bold move. She had never visited the library, museum or the art gallery except for a school excursion to the museum aeons ago and these institutions were as far from her lifestyle as a trip to the moon. After discovering the big city bookshops, however, and becoming even a little confident of her place in them, she found the courage, after seeing a poster in one about a function at the State Library, to have a look and see what it was like.

Sitting in the Swanson Street tram for the short ride to the library, Monica pondered on the many changes in her life in such a short period of time. Here she was, ordinary old Mon, on her way to the State Library. One year ago, if anyone had suggested this occurrence might take place, she would have scoffed at the ridiculousness of the idea. As if. But here she was, neatly attired in a smart grey woollen suit with a brightly coloured scarf draped nonchalantly over one shoulder, off to the library. She wondered if Mrs Next Door went to the State Library and how often and what might she wear. Certainly she would be smartly dressed to visit a Government Building.

When the tram stopped, however, and Monica was

faced with the big imposing marble building, she nearly changed her mind. What on earth was she thinking of? Just who did she think she was? What right had she, Monica, to go into that massive, terrifying building? But after all she was there, the tram had moved on and what a fool she would feel to cross the tracks and stand waiting for the tram back. Resolutely she approached the sliding glass doors and with more courage than she thought she was capable of, stepped through as they opened.

For a moment, panicking, she found herself trapped between the door that automatically closed behind her and another set of glass doors that were shut. Within seconds though they opened and she moved forward into the large foyer where she was faced by an imposing desk with a girl behind it and security men seemingly everywhere. What to do? She wanted to run back through those glass doors but was blocked now by people behind her, moving forward, past the desk and through a small security section that reminded her of those she'd seen in airport movies. Then the weight of people dispersed, pushing past her reluctant body and she was left standing looking at hundreds of computers, not books but computers, with people sitting gazing earnestly at the screens, some even seemingly asleep.

This was not what she had imagined at all; she had imagined a sort-of ultra-large bookshop. Not computers. Suddenly, aghast at her audacity, it was all too much for her and she turned and nearly ran to the glass doors where she had to wait with several other people, her heart pounding, until the doors opened and she could leave the marble building and stand to the side of the door in the fresh air and catch her breath.

Monica felt ashamed and stupid. Well, that's what she was, wasn't it, stupid? Furious at her own inadequacy, she caught the next tram back to the shops and although she was in no mood to meander about the stores, she bought herself a set of satin sheets and pillowcases which she'd been promising herself since she first pleasured herself after the day of the red dress. If she could not be smart and clever she would at least be sensual, she fumed, and feeling anything but sensual she drove home, nearly in tears, where she threw the precious sheets on a chair and plonked herself in front of the tele with cake and coffee.

Monica's forays into sensual pleasure had been few and far between since she first discovered the joy of orgasm. The act made her feel guilty and slightly disgusted when she thought about it afterwards, but caught in the moment of sensual abandonment, usually instigated by the touch of a fabric, she found herself carried away to a height of pleasure that she always thought could never happen again. She had often imagined sleeping alone in the bed with satin sheets and to date had denied herself that pleasure, but, disappointed to her core about the library, she'd bought them out of pique, although they had not been allowed for in the budget.

After a snooze on the couch in front of the tele, feeling a little better, she made up the bed ready for the evening. Running her hands over the smooth satin she decided to go out to the verandah after all. For the first time since the afternoon ritual had begun she doubted the whole stupid business on the way home from the library and had decided not to go out that day. But the satin, the glorious, luxurious, smooth satin won her over and underneath the dark green woollen skirt and gold roll-neck jumper that she'd put aside for today she wore a new silk petticoat that she'd been saving for a special day. Slipping the soft silk over and down her body after her shower, with no bra, made her feel capable and confident again. She had only to hope that next-door would be wearing the same loose jumper for most of her clothes demanded a bra.

The silk petticoat, like the sheets, had been of her own choosing and wearing it today when she needed a bit of a lift was like hiding something naughty from the teacher and it made her feel good. Of course, she well knew, that Mrs Next Door probably wore silk underwear all the time but nevertheless this was Monica's secret and she felt good about it.

And so the days slipped by, the afternoon sojourn the most important time of the day for both women. They had still never spoken to one another but Miss Trante's raised glass and raised eyes spoke volumes when Monica took her place on the couch with the correct clothes and correct wine and book. Both women were happy; Miss Trante, still in charge and leading Monica gradually, through her envelopes in the letter box, felt gratified and generous to the extreme. Monica, learning more each day from her wondrous books, not to mention the fashion and good taste from her neighbour, was discovering a part of herself that she had never acknowledged and was perfectly happy to assume the position of follower. Life was good for the two ageing women, hidden away from the world by bricks and mortar and indifference.

X

The white sandals

SHARP at three-thirty, Monica stepped out to the verandah. She had with her their latest book and a fine crystal goblet of white wine which she placed carefully on the small table by the couch before settling back against the leather and velvet cushions. Only then did she raise her eyes and look across to the opposite verandah.

It was Thursday, so she had chosen to wear a smartly knitted dark green skirt and a bright floral silk top with a shirt collar and long sleeves buttoned neatly at her wrists. The outfit was a bit of a gamble, but she was counting on the brightness of the afternoon sun and the general well-being of the fine spring weather and was sure she had made the right choice.

To her astonishment the verandah opposite her own was empty. She checked her watch unobtrusively as possible, in case she might be caught in the act, but she hadn't made a mistake; it was a few minutes passed three-thirty. She knew her watch was right. She checked it every day against the ABC radio at noon and it had not failed her yet.

Well, she thought, things can go wrong. A ladder in a stocking, a loose button. She took a small sip of her wine, replacing the glass on the table. She opened her book, carefully placing the oriental bookmark on the couch beside her and began to read. Two or three paragraphs into it, she glanced up again. Nobody. Back to the book. Check the watch. Seven minutes. Read a bit longer. Another small

sip. Read again. How hard it was to concentrate!

A half hour passed and still she had not come out. How odd. This had never happened before. Monica had several sips of her wine, looking over at the verandah the whole time, as if willing her to come out. Nothing. What would she do? What could she do?

At half past four Monica walked over to the brick wall and listened. There were no sounds coming from the house except for the radio, tastefully low, the sliding glass door was not even open, she noted. Suddenly aware she might get caught peering over the wall, she returned quickly to her couch where she sat again and began re-reading the chapter that she'd started earlier, but had not absorbed. Afraid, in a way, now to look, she listened carefully for the sound of the sliding door, or a glass on a table or the scuff or a shoe. Nothing.

At quarter to five, her glass empty now, Monica went into the kitchen and refilled it. She never had before, on the verandah. One glass sipped slowly, had been the norm. But today, today she needed it. Back on the couch, staring across the brick wall to the opposite verandah, Monica slowly drank the second wine.

What if she was sick? What if she was dead? Or worse, Monica thought with horror, what if she'd gone out?

Monica wondered if she dare go over there and knock on the door.

Of course not, she'd look such a fool. She checked her watch again. Five o'clock! Time to go in already.

Upset beyond description, she picked up her book, swilled the last dregs in the glass and went inside. Part of her was furious, part worried and puzzled.

Methodically she changed into her dressing gown, carefully hanging the pretty blouse on a hanger which she hooked over the back of a chair. The skirt she spread out neatly on top of a tan one already lying on the table.

As she pushed her pantyhose down she suddenly pulled at them in frustration, nearly tripping herself up.

She threw them angrily on the floor.

Well bugger it, she thought. She'd been looking forward to a frozen roast pork dinner and now she didn't feel like eating anything. Where the hell was that bloody woman! She glanced at the variety of clothing hanging about the dinette and lying on the table. Quite a collection. For what? She thought in fury. For what? And how was she supposed to get through until three-thirty tomorrow, she questioned. No bloody idea.

Standing there in her undies and dressing-gown, her whole world upside down, she realised that she'd never be able to sleep. She'd never be able to wait until tomorrow afternoon. Her old placid, patient self had disappeared somewhere since the verandah business. She lived now in a place of anticipation, excitement and pleasure. Her world now, as much as she'd settled into the routine of it, was different and sometimes even a bit scary.

Well, she thought, as soon as it begins to get a bit dark, when everyone would be having tea, she'd go and knock on the sliding door. But why wait, why not go straight away? She shuddered. She didn't want to go at all. Never had she set foot on her neighbour's property and the thought terrified her. No, she'd wait until tomorrow. Somehow. Tightening her mouth she realised that the whole stupid situation was not her fault anyway. She'd gone out at 3.30.

Blow it.

She went to the freezer, took out her pork roast and put it in the microwave. She saw no reason now why her night should be spoiled. Setting the folding tray up by her chair in the lounge and putting on the tele, Monica calmed a little, her worry turning to scorn.

She ate her roast when it was ready, had a coffee and three chocolate biscuits, watched tele until 9.30 and went to bed.

Next morning, eyeing her special clothes that cluttered the dinette as she made her morning cuppa, she refused to let herself get cross again about the previous afternoon. Perhaps she wouldn't go out to the verandah herself to-day, she thought with a nasty smile. But she knew she couldn't do it. So she went about her usual routine, spent some time in the warm morning sun working in the garden and, deciding on the mauve and pink dress to match the fuchsias, she stepped out to the verandah at exactly three-thirty.

As usual, she had her book and a glass of white wine. As usual, she seated herself on the lounge before looking up and across at the opposite verandah. Once again, there was nobody there.

Something is definitely wrong, thought Monica, deciding that if she was not out in half an hour she'd go and see.

Half an hour passed. Nothing.

Worried about her original decision now the time had come, Monica picked up her wine and drank the lot for courage. Yes, she could do this. She removed the book from her lap, walked over as far as the brick fence and stopped. Once over that fence she would be committed. From where she stood she could see that the sliding door was still closed, but the soft sound of the radio was still there. Blow it, she thought, lifting one leg and going side-ways over the low fence. She stepped on to the blue and white tiles and knocked softly on the glass door.

No answer. She knocked harder, quite loudly in fact. So loudly that she stepped quickly back from the door in shock. What if the woman came out angrily with a "what the devil do you want"or "I'm not playing your stupid game anymore, go away." Or even simply opened the door and stared at her without saying a word. She knew she would die on the spot. But Monica had to know and with a stoic bravery and still no answer after waiting for about two minutes, she tried the door and finding it un-locked, she stepped inside.

"Hello there," she called hesitantly to the empty room in front of her. Well, hardly empty, she thought, surveying the beautiful furnishings in front of her. A real Aladdin's cave.

Hesitantly she ran her hand over the French polished dining table in front of her and gently touched the top of one of the tapestry chairs. The sideboard on her right was covered in beautiful pottery and filled, behind its glass doors, with an array of crystal glasses and jugs, the likes of which she'd never seen before. A three-quarter high wall, also with beautiful pottery pieces along the top, ran behind the sideboard and probably hid a kitchen she surmised.

The entire length of the outside wall (that which faced Monica's house) was one gigantic bookshelf, reaching from the floor to about half a metre from the ceiling. Along the top of the bookshelf sat a collection of stunning statues of various heights and materials, each one worthy of long appreciation. Monica, though, dismissing these in one glance, was awe-struck by the hundreds of books that were housed in the beautiful shelving. The timber shelves were not simply laid out methodically but each section was of a different height and width. The shelves, empty, would have been an artwork in themselves so beautifully were they constructed. But the books. The books. Hundreds and hundreds; thin ones, tall ones, fat ones, small ones, new ones and very old ones. Every coloured spine imaginable. How many years of reading, Monica wondered? What stories could they all hold? She had no idea how long she stood there. In front of the books. Envious to the extreme. Then she heard a faint sound in the quietness and had to move.

"Hello," she called again, stepping further into the house, into the open lounge area now, with comfy leather chairs and a stunning centre oriental rug. Listening, while taking in the stereo unit and television set encased in an attractive carved wooden unit, she thought she heard a small sound from upstairs. Boldly starting up the carpeted stairs, Monica realised with some surprise that she was actually inside the house. Should she run back to the safety of her own verandah, she queried for an instant, then hearing another quiet sound, a moan she thought, she continued up the stairs to a landing where there were two bedroom doors, one open. Through the open door she could see a double bed with a skirt and blouse laid out ready, the green skirt and the silk floral blouse. Yesterday's, she thought with a shock, but pleased too that her choice had been correct. She stepped into the room and was immediately aware of an open door to her right; the bathroom obviously, with a cream tiled floor and a towel rack partly visible behind the door. Matching cream towels, she noted, as she stepped into the doorway and saw the woman lying on her back on the floor, naked and old.

Miss Trante, raising her eyes to glimpse Monica in the doorway, realised that she'd been found. "Help,"she moaned in a quiet cracked voice, her mouth dry from the lack of water. She couldn't swing her head around, the pain of movement too great. It had taken every ounce of strength she'd had to force herself to roll from her stomach where she'd fallen. The pain then had made her pass out and she was fearful of it happening again.

Seeing the woman lying there so thin and helpless, without thinking, Monica reached down and with one swift movement, slipping her hands under the bony shoulders to the underarms, she lifted the head and torso up from the floor. The woman screamed.

"Don't move me, you stupid cow," she groaned viciously. "I've got a broken hip."

Stupid cow.

Stupid cow.

Stupid cow.

The verandah game had all been a joke. The whole time, Monica realised, this old woman had been playing her like a fish. Stupid cow.

Without a word Monica let go of the injured woman and winced a little as the body dropped back on to the tiles, the head hitting the floor with a dull cracking sound. She stood there, very still, for quite a few minutes, looking down at her mentor with disgust. The woman was quiet now, her eyes glazed with shock, mouth open, but she was still breathing. Monica watched the bony rib cage move slowly up and down.

Taking a deep breath, Monica turned and left the bathroom and the woman. With her she took the two cream towels into the bedroom where she folded them neatly and put them on the bottom of the bed. Then, as an afterthought, she returned to the room, stepped over the woman to the small open window and shut it thoroughly, wiping the handle with her cuff. Without even glancing downwards, she moved back out of the bathroom and pulled the door firmly shut behind her, using the soft fabric of her skirt to hold the door handle and turned and left the room. The old woman would be unable to pull herself up without the towels for leverage and it would be highly unlikely that she could ever reach the door handle. She could stay there and rot, thought Monica.

On the landing, about to head down the stairs, Monica suddenly remembered the clothes. She had to have a look in the wardrobe. And she did.

The wardrobe covered the entire length of the outside wall and had mirrored doors, making the room look twice its size. The woman's clothes were spread spaciously along the rack to avoid crushing and all of the coat hangers, except of course those with clips for skirts and slacks, were covered in soft fabric and left no bumps in the shoulders of the smart jackets and dresses. There was a whole compartment for shoes with a shoe-rack included, each pair laid out neatly. Monica was very interested in the shoes. It had been difficult across the distance between the verandahs to see the shoes properly.

Monica sat on the soft carpet and admired the shoes. Such nice leathers and suedes. Some with small heels, some flat. Hesitantly she reached out and touched a particularly nice pair of black suedes and, moving one shoe a fraction, she saw a shoe box behind the rack, obviously new. She pulled it out. Inside, still cosseted in soft tissue paper, were a smart, white summer pair of sandals, with soft straps and small heel. Lovely, thought Monica. She noticed a receipt tucked inside the box and decided to take box and contents home with her. The name of the shoe shop would be there and although the sandals themselves would probably be too small for her she'd be able to go to the shop and buy the same style in her own size. She tucked the shoe box under her arm, closed the wardrobe door and went downstairs.

The radio was still on. After a bit of searching she located the volume knob on the complicated stereo unit and turned the volume up a fraction. Self-consciously she once again gripped the knob with her dress hem. Foolish, she thought, the woman's eventual death could only be construed as a natural fall, but still, she must be careful.

Leaving the house immediately, she closed the sliding door behind her and wiped the edge of that. She stood on HER verandah for a while, then on impulse sat on the couch where SHE had sat. Softer than her own.

Sitting hidden away from neighbours, she looked across at her own verandah and imagined seeing herself sitting there. But the game was over. What would she live for now? The afternoons had given her a purpose and an excitement and pleasure that she was loathe to lose. She found herself close to tears and was disappointed at her own weakness. Pulling herself together with a sniff she took another look at her verandah from this new point of view. How strange her life had become. Glancing down at the tiles she realised for the first time that they were actually different from her own, the pattern more delicate and finely painted. Other than that and the amazing softness of the couch, there was virtually no difference. She had done well, she congratulated herself, and lulled by the music coming from the house, she found herself settling comfortably back into the couch, staring across at her own verandah waiting for herself to come out from the sliding doors. She could hear no sound from the house except for the radio. Good.

Suddenly, with a start, she realised how odd these verandahs might look to anybody who might discover Her upstairs. And that was inevitable, she had to admit. She had at least a week, she figured, depending on how much mail might build-up in the letter box and how many phone calls went unanswered. She had absolutely no idea if the phone in this house ever rang, or rang non-stop. Other than the verandah, she realised, she knew absolutely nothing about her neighbour or her life. But still, a week at least she thought, and sitting there on her couch her practical side came to the fore and she began to plan how she could quickly alter the sameness of the verandahs. Others would not, could not, understand and she had no wish to be tied to this woman anymore, in life or in death.

She rose, taking her shoe box and the pot from the round glass table. Stepping carefully over the fence after checking that there was nobody in sight on the front footpath, she returned to her kitchen where she put the pot in a cupboard, took the shoe box to the bedroom for later, then, pouring a glass of wine, she went out and sat on her own verandah to think. The whole neighbouring verandah would have to change and she would have to do it quickly. She had several hours to wait until dark to start, the late summer evenings stretching now until nine o'clock or so.

Finishing her wine she went inside to make a sandwich and, entering the dinette, she was faced with all of her good clothes cluttering the entire room.

Furious, she decided to put them away immediately. Carrying a few at a time and hanging them carefully in the wardrobe she wondered at her own foolishness. To be taken in and taken over by that horrible woman. Idly she wondered if she was still alive. She had no idea how long it took to die without food or water and she'd had that nasty bump on the head as well. Serves her right, thought Monica. I'm not even going to check until tomorrow. Still smarting from "stupid cow". I'll show you who's a stupid cow.

The clothing away, with a mental note to buy some nice coat hangers, she sat at her dinette table. Pine, she realised for the first time, thinking of the beautiful one next door. Well pine would do her, she thought, pleased to have the luxury of sitting at the table again after such a long time. She unrolled the local monthly paper she'd picked up from the lawn and luxuriously spread it open to read while she ate her sandwich. Leafing through, she noticed a small ad for a builder; additions, minor alterations, no job too small. A picture popped into her head of an enclosed verandah. another cream brick wall at the end, blocking off next door for good and maybe glass along the back so winter wouldn't limit its use. Something to think about.

She tucked the idea away and continued reading the paper. The paper! Next door's would be lying about in her front yard. A noticeable thing. Dare she creep out tonight and get it? She didn't like the idea. She could be seen at the front of the house from the street. She'd see how she felt tonight.

At nine o'clock, after listening for any unusual noises or activity in the area, she hopped over the fence to next door's verandah. She stood for a while listening at the sliding doors hearing nothing but the radio. Quickly she lifted the glass out of the round table, heaved it over the fence and carried it down to Frank's shed. It was heavier than she'd imagined and puffing, she left it for the moment resting against the nearest wall making a mental note to cover it with something later. Then she brought the iron table itself, lighter than the glass and easy enough to swing over the low bricks, and stood it upside down on Frank's side of the verandah. A couple of bits of old wood on top of that and it'd just look like more junk. The small end table by the couch she could easily manage in one go, that also relegated to the shed. Swinging the wrought-iron chair over the fence, she slipped it under her own table, where it sat comfortably, as if it had been there forever.

She knew, strong as she was, that she couldn't move the heavy couch over the fence. Taking an old checked blanket from the linen cupboard the threw it over the couch, tucking it firmly along the back against the bricks and pushing it in place along the back of the seat. The velvet cushions went back to her own couch, making it look more luxurious than ever.

The two big blue pots with the Kentia palms would be a problem. Far too heavy to move, even for her. Tomorrow, she decided, she'd do something with them tomorrow.

Already though, without the glass tables and with the couch looking completely different, next door's verandah was far removed from her own. Once those damned Kentias were moved, any likeness, other than similar tiles, would virtually disappear.

Quietly Monica crept along the narrow space between the two houses and reaching the front garden checked to see if anybody was about. With nobody to be seen, she hopped over the wall into next door's front yard and quickly found the local paper which was lying on the lawn near a thick ground cover. She kicked the paper between the branches of the plant where it was out of sight and quietly returned to the back of the houses where she became instantly aware, even in the darkness of the evening, that the similarity of the gardens was powerfully obvious. That would have to change. She'd begin tomorrow.

She had a lot to do tomorrow. Maybe ring that builder perhaps. Buy a pile of plants and pots and potting soil to clutter up next door's immaculate tiles and move those bloody Kentia palms. Begin changing and replanning her whole back yard. Now that was a real nuisance, she'd become accustomed to it as it was, but it had to be done. And she must buy some covered coat-hangers for her clothes.

But for now, sleep. She found she was amazingly tired and noted that it was past eleven, late for her, Nevertheless, out of sheer stubbornness and a strange rebellion, because she hadn't got around to reading on the verandah today, she read for half an hour before switching off the light and falling asleep.

Monica slept until 9.30, as was her habit. Stretching under the doona, remembering the previous day, she lay there for some time planning her new backyard in her mind. When she was satisfied with the changes she rose, dressed in old clothes, had one cup of coffee and went immediately out the back and with the help of her large gardening fork pulled up every shrub that she'd planted the year before and threw them on the compost. The geranium by the verandah came out too and that was a shame; it was such a pretty red. Before that, too, was relegated to the compost, Monica cut all the flowering stems and took them inside where she arranged them in a vase and placed it in the centre of the now clear dining table. Nice, she thought, admiring it, very nice. In a day or two, when she had more time, she'd cut up all those shrubs with her secateurs and dig them into the compost. For now though they were out and even though her backyard looked a mess it was completely unlike that of next door. The young gums, hardly rooted, came out easily. A shame, she thought, because she was rather fond of natives. Well, she would get some wattles, she decided, and they could go right along the iron fence nearly to the compost heap. With a row across the back just leaving room for the fruit trees.

She was becoming quite excited now. The different yellows of the flowers and varying times of the year that they were in bloom would mean a picture from her verandah. The lawn could be extended back to the wattles. Oh, it would be lovely.

After a quick lunch and a shower she changed into tidy clothes to go shopping. She was only going to the mall and the nearby nursery so she didn't need to wear her best.

She would change again before 3.30, she decided, simply to please herself. She would never have to stress about choosing the right clothes ever again. Looking back she could hardly believe what a worry it had been every single day and how silly she had been to care what that old bag next door would be wearing. Well, she could choose now. And forever.

Feeling fresh and in control, Monica drove to the nursery, quite excited about choosing her wattles. Four different types, she figured, and three of each. That allowed seven along the fence and five across the back. They were fast growing trees too, so if she bought well established plants they'd make quite a display fairly quickly around the edges of the lawn that she was planning to extend. Imagining it all in her head, she supposed she really ought to put a couple down the side of Frank's shed, which was the third side to the back lawn, but since she couldn't see that from the verandah she decided not to bother.

At the nursery she chose the wattles that she wanted and arranged for them to be delivered. Although she was happy enough to hook up the trailer and drive it, she wasn't good at backing and couldn't be bothered even trying. She had enough to do as it was. Those big palms for a start. She must move them tonight. Planning, planning in her head she bought a bag of potting soil, half a dozen largish empty plastic pots and eight small, cheap shrubs in smaller pots. These she could take in the boot ready for tonight. Then to the mall.

For the first time since her original introduction to the bookshop she could wander through aisle after aisle and choose whatever books took her fancy. No instructions from next door today. Certainly she had been buying an extra book or two now and then since she'd become enthralled with reading, but each time she'd chosen something for herself she'd been riddled with guilt. What if the book wasn't good enough? What if that old bat next door somehow found out what she'd chosen? But now, now she could please herself entirely.

Like a child in a lolly shop, she picked books up and read the back and a page or two and put them down. So many to chose from. She would have to buy another bookshelf for herself, for the lounge. Not yet though. Later. Another biography for now, she eventually decided, and a thriller. She had found that she'd enjoyed most of the biographies; learning about other people's lives with amazement. The thriller was just for fun. She loved whodunits.

Pleased with her book purchases, she treated herself to coffee and Danish in the now familiar little coffee shop and headed home to get ready for her afternoon on the verandah.

At 3.30, clothes changed and tidy, she stepped out to the verandah with her glass and her new biography. Seated comfortably against the extra cushions she looked across at the other verandah. The couch was there, looking completely different with the rug over it and the two palms in their blue pots. It looked empty and ordinary. Even though this had been her own doing she felt disappointed. Sad even. Her afternoons were ruined now and crossly she took the book and wine inside. She tipped the wine down the sink and plonked the book on the dinette table. Might as well have a rest, she thought, ready for tonight. Nothing else to do.

Annoyed, grumpy and rubbing her lower back with one hand, Monica stomped along the passage to the bedroom. She spotted the shoe box from next door on the corner chair and sitting on the bed she lifted the lid and carefully spread the tissue paper to reveal the white sandals. Her bad mood forgotten, she lifted one out and held it carefully. Beautiful. Two sizes too small, but she could still get a pair for herself. Rummaging in the box for the receipt, pulling the tissue out, she found a flat parcel at the bottom of the box, also wrapped in tissue. She pulled at the soft paper, tearing it where it had been stuck down with tape, and dozens of hundred-dollar bills flew out all over the bed and the floor. Monica froze. Money. She'd only meant to take the shoes. She was not a thief. But there it was. On her bed. Lots of it.

Slowly Monica collected all the notes and stacked them in a pile on the doona, counting as she went. Sixteen thousand dollars. She counted again. Yes, sixteen thousand dollars. What a thing! She re-wrapped the money as best she could in the torn paper, put it in the bottom of the box and arranged the sandals in their own tissue on the top. Firmly she closed the lid and put the box at the back of her own wardrobe behind her own shoes. She took off her good clothes and lay on top of the bed, naked. Thinking. After some time, aware of the advancing cool of the late spring evening, she popped under the doona and slept for several hours.

It was nearly dark when she awoke, stiff and sore again and hungry. She remembered the money. She'd think about that later. Tomorrow. Tonight she had work to do.

Feeling quite cheery, dressed again in her dirty work clothes, she made a strong cup of instant coffee and heated a frozen lasagne in the microwave. Eating at the table again, with the geraniums, oh what a joy, she once again turned to the paper, finding the builders' advertisement and re-reading it carefully. Yes, she'd decided already, she realised, she'd give them a ring and get a quote.

With new energy, noting it had become dark outside, she put on her rubber gloves and unloaded the pots and soil from the car boot, carrying a load at a time and popping them over the low fence. She stepped quietly over it herself and on to the verandah, listening at the door for sounds. Only the radio.

Quietly, sliding the glass door across by the handle with her gloves, she moved into the living room and listened. Still only the radio. Unsure of herself with the stairs in the dark, she decided to put a light on. Passers-by, unless they actually came and peered through the window, which was unlikely, would take little notice of lights going on and off. After a time she found the light switch for the lounge, switched it on and made her way up the stairs. She also put the bedroom light on, the switch much easier to find, and stood and looked at the bathroom door. Still shut. Good. She was turning to leave when she saw the cream towels that she'd put on the bed. Perhaps one of them should go back in the bathroom, she thought, the more obvious place to dry oneself. But that meant opening the door and she didn't want to. She had been stupid to take them out in the first place, but she hadn't wanted her using them to pull herself up to the door knob. Two days now, Or three?

Monica stood next to the bathroom door, her gloved hand tentatively around the doorknob. There was no smell noticeable in the bedroom, she noted. Perhaps the old girl was still alive. Clenching her jaw tightly she turned the handle and opened the door a fraction. Instantly she was hit by the stench of defecation. She shut the door quickly. What she had seen of the woman suggested that she hadn't moved, but Monica was still not sure if she was dead or not, perhaps only having emptied her bladder and bowel. What to do? She reached over to the bed and grabbed one towel which she unfolded and screwed up a bit. Holding her breath and averting her eyes she quickly opened the door, threw the towel on the floor next to the woman and shut it again with a bang. The noise in the quiet house made her jump. Switching off the bedroom light she moved quickly down the stairs where she also switched of the living room light and took herself out to the verandah, sliding the door shut behind her.

She was glad to be out of the house. She hated everything to do with that woman now and was impatient to finish her work and be done with the whole place. She decided then and there that she wouldn't go back inside again for any reason. She was done with her.

Determined to be finished now, Monica looked at the palms in the big, heavy blue pots. Far too difficult to lift over the low brick wall even though she was a strong woman. With wisdom that she didn't know she possessed, she went back to Frank's side of the verandah and found a wide plank that she could use like a see-saw, balanced over the lowest edge of the wall. Puffing a bit, she slowly manoeuvered the first heavy pot over to the timber sliding at tipping it a little at a time. Once there she tipped it on its side and rolled it up to the top of the parapet. Holding it carefully in place she hopped over the fence and pushed the other end of the timber to the ground so that she could roll the heavy pot down to the edge of her verandah. The weight of the first pot took her by surprise and it rolled too quickly, falling off the timber and smashing on the ground. Undeterred she shook as much dirt from the roots as she could and lugged the palm down to the compost heap to be cut up later. The broken pieces of pot she collected and took around to Frank's side of the verandah. What a mess that was now. Still, she didn't have to look at it except on washing days when she needed to use the laundry door which opened on to that side. Shrugging her shoulders she decided in the future she'd carry the laundry basket out through the dinette. Bugger the messy verandah.

The second blue pot was far easier. This time she was prepared for the weight and was able to manoeuvre it safely down beside the verandah. From there, panting a bit now, Monica swung one side up on to her tiles and then the other. Bit by bit she edged it across the verandah to the sliding door and placed it next to the fixed glass so that it sat sweetly in the corner between the door and the couch.

Ready for a rest by now but anxious to be finished, Monica returned next door where she moved the empty pots and small potted shrubs on to the verandah. The bag of potting mix was heavy and awkward and as she dropped it on to the tiles it split open. Perfect, thought Monica. A wonderfully messy, plain old back verandah. Wouldn't herself upstairs be furious if she could see it. She plopped down on the couch for a moment, exhausted. Looking across at her own verandah, with light spilling out from the dinette and kitchen windows, she was thrilled. The extra palm, extra cushions and extra chair filled it in beautifully. How exotic it looked. And so tasteful.

Climbing back over the fence and leaving next-door for the last time, Monica nearly laughed out loud. Only twelve months ago she'd looked over that tin fence and seen such a verandah. Now it was hers and hers alone. It belonged to her and she to it. Although very weary with a bugger of a backache, Monica had to celebrate. She went inside and poured herself a glass of wine, glancing at the clock. Eleven-thirty. Goodness. She never had a wine at night, only in the afternoons, but tonight her new wondrous verandah deserved it. Sitting there on the couch in the quietness of the night, sipping her wine, Monica looked across at next door's empty verandah. Just a house with a verandah on the back corner. Ordinary. And silent. From where she sat she couldn't even hear the radio. Pleased with her day, Monica finished the wine and went to bed, falling asleep quickly, her face relaxed and at peace.

Four weeks later, should anyone have gone down the side of Miss Trante's house to the back they would have seen a very ordinary yard, unwatered and in need of care and a tiled back verandah with a couch of some sort covered with a blanket and a heap of pots and potting soil spread about with a few small dying plants, obviously waiting to go in the garden. With all the dried leaves that had blown into the verandah, one might think that the owner of the house was either away or too busy to care about the garden

If one should look across the low brick wall to the neighbouring house all one would see would be a cream brick wall, extending now right to the back of the verandah, and lawn, shed and wattle trees out the back.

But nobody went to the back of Miss Trante's house. If anybody visited at all, after getting no answer at the front door and not being able to see if her car was there because the garage roll-a-door was down as usual, they left.

The only person that might step between the two houses would be the electricity man to read the meters, which were anyway close to the front of the houses on the side walls. If it were noted that very little electricity had been used it would mean nothing, people travelling and so forth all the time. Only when the bill was overdue and then long overdue might someone show concern or else the power would simply be disconnected after a warning by mail.

The housing estate clattered and sang like it usually did, cars driving in and out, children roller-blading around the streets shouting and laughing. Nobody took any notice at all of the two houses where the oldies lived. Monica's car could sometimes be seen coming and going and a builder's van and glass truck had been and gone, which was nothing out of the ordinary with young families extending all the time. The small cliques that formed in the estate, probably through children attending different schools, were seldom neighbours and a person could live or die in this environment without being noticed at all.

AT 3.30 exactly, Monica stepped out on to her verandah. She put her crystal goblet of fine wine, a semillon, carefully on the small table and sat with her book on the white couch, adjusting the soft cushions around her back. Taking the oriental-looking book-mark from the book, the latest best-selling novel according to the assistant in the bookshop, she placed it on her lap, crossed her ankles and raised her eyes to her reflection in the mirrored wall at the opposite end of the verandah. The mirror, inspired by the mirrored wardrobe in next-door's bedroom, covered the entire new cream brick wall that filled in the end of the verandah.

Monica had opened the concertina glass doors that ran along the back of the verandah earlier in the day so that the air in the verandah was cool and scented by the wattles. The man who had come to install the big mirror had suggested this type of glass door to fill in the verandah room.

"Ah, keep 'em open in summer," he'd said, "and shut 'em up in winter. Best of both worlds."

Monica had to admit that he was right. She could have an open verandah or a glassed-in room. She was thrilled.

Monica raised her crystal goblet to her own reflection. There she sat, resplendent in a short-sleeved silk shirt-dress of turquoise, green and white, chosen for the late spring warmth and to complement her three thriving palms in their blue pots. On her feet she wore a new pair of white sandals, soft leather with a small heel. She glanced briefly at the small blue pot on the round glass table, took a sip of wine, and began to read.

THE END